KILL BETH

JON COHN

To Dad. I miss you.

ALSO BY JON COHN

The Island Mother

Slashtag

Try Not To Die On Slashtag

Everything Is Temporary

Contents

Spontaneous Writing: Session 1

Carrots and cheese, carrots and cheese,
Why did you agree to writing these?
You shouldn't have come home, you should have said no
Maybe it's not too late to pack up and go.
You can't be here, too much fear
There's something in the atmosphere
Carrots and carrots and carrots and cheese,
The world is falling like Seattle's leaves
Its cardinal sin, you've broken the rule
Coming back to this playhouse, you were a fool
This place is cursed, bad memories abound
Wherever you go, that's where you're found
What are you doing, Mike? this is all wrong
And why are you rhyming? This isn't a song
Carrots and cheese, carrots and cheese,
Someone get me out of here please
You're spinning out now, completely a mess,
There's only one way out, and that's to KILL BETH.

Chapter 1

My alarm goes off at 6:35 a.m. I always set it at least fifteen minutes earlier than necessary. Sometimes more. Extra padding means less anxiety, especially on days like this, when I have an appointment with my therapist.

It only takes fifteen minutes to get showered and dressed. I keep my hair extremely short so it will look fine without me needing to labor over a mirror. That would add an unknown and unwanted variable to my routine.

Before leaving my apartment, I give myself one minute to thumb every knob on the stove, making sure they are off, then open and shut the fridge to guarantee the seal is still intact. If I don't, a voice in my head will constantly assault me with worries about my food spoiling or coming home to a burning building. I can't help but check for safety every time I pass. It probably accounts for at least three minutes of wasted time per week.

The nearby bakery is a five-minute walk, but I add an extra minute both ways to account for potential crosswalk wait time. I give myself ten minutes to order and receive my latte and blueberry muffin, which I eat on the return trip to Greenwood Terrace.

Despite the name, the building is shingled with slats of splintered dark wood. All the units in the three-story complex are street-facing, with the walkways outdoors, like a motel. The untreated cracks in the façade make perfect hiding spots for colonies of spiders, beetles, centipedes, and any other assortment of creepy-crawlies. I never touch these walls while I travel to and from my temporary home.

My assigned apartment is 3A—a third-floor corner unit. When I go up or down any set of stairs, I always skip a step, unless there are an uneven number, which would result in me taking two consecutive stairs at the end of my flight. That is no good. In that case, I will climb onto the first step and use every other one so I can hit the landing properly. It only takes me one try to learn a stair set's pattern for life, but I still take note of it every time.

The unit supplied to me by the theater is spartan, with a firm bed—good—a firm couch—bad—a TV, a cramped bathroom, a kitchenette, a fireplace, several old but sturdy cabinets and drawers for my things, and a nook where I like to work on my laptop.

My muffin is already eaten by the time I'm through the door. I check my phone: 7:12 a.m. Still plenty of time before my 7:30 Zoom appointment. After checking the stove knobs and fridge, I finish my drink, brush my teeth to make sure I have no foreign objects stuck in there, wash my hands of any potentially sticky muffin residue, and double-check that every item I need for the day is correctly organized in my shoulder bag.

Once on my laptop, I make sure my Wi-Fi connection is steady, ensure my wireless headphones are fully charged and properly synced to the computer—I have wired backups in a bedside drawer, just in case—then email a document to Dr. Jules ahead of our call. I also print the page out and have it next to the computer. Having everything in hard copy just feels better.

For the remaining time, I sit, staring at the screen and ruminating in a spiral of the same twenty or so thoughts which always plague me before a session.

Of course, I make sure I'm in the Zoom waiting room at least three minutes ahead of our appointment time. Dr. Jules, my therapist, is never early, but it makes me feel more at ease knowing she is aware that I am punctual and ready for our twice-weekly session.

An ever-present tightness eases off my chest when her video takes over my screen. There is a cool comfort in recognizing the shelves behind her, always filled with the same books, and the tall Monstera plant bathing in the sun of her New York apartment. As a constantly traveling theater director who lives out of a set of suitcases, I find the background of her office more like a home than anywhere I stay.

There is also a calm associated with Dr. Jules's presence. Her silver-stranded hair always maintains the same form and length. Her attire is professional—one of eight blouses she has worn to work in the last three years—and her jewelry is limited to her wedding ring—modest but still noticeable.

"Good morning, Mike," she says with clinical warmth. I'm sure she greets all her patients with the same tone, but feeling like she is happy to see me helps my mind ease into the session. "How's Seattle treating you this week?"

"I'm doing okay." It is only a partial lie, though I always experience more worry in the early and late hours of the day. By ten, I will probably be too focused on work to get anxious. "Did you get my email?"

She nods. "I did, and I just opened it up. Give me a minute to read it through, and then we can talk."

I tap my heel rapidly against the carpet. Restless leg. My heartbeat shudders while I stare intently at her face, searching for clues as to how she is interpreting my first attempt at spontaneous writing.

A hint of a smile. The slightest chortle of a laugh blows from her nose.

Which part is she laughing at?

She indicates she is finished when her eyes return to a space just below the camera, where I guess either my face or hers is located on her screen.

I hurry before she has a chance to say anything, needing her to understand, first and foremost, that I tried my best to do the assignment properly.

"I know I made the whole thing rhyme. I couldn't help it."

"That's perfectly fine. We know that pattern-seeking behavior is a symptom of your obsessive-compulsive disorder. As long as it's part of your stream of consciousness, there's no wrong way to practice spontaneous writing."

"I know. I just remembered you had stressed that I try to clear my head and type without purpose, and I worried rhyming would make it seem like I was writing with intent or collecting my thoughts first."

Dr. Jules once again gives me her practiced smile. She gently shakes her head. "You're a very creative person, Mike, and extremely quick on your feet. For some people, I might see a rhyme scheme as an indicator of premeditation, but I'm not at all surprised to see you subconsciously expressing raw thoughts this way. The goal here isn't to cure you of your obsessive tendencies; it's to get you to express your subconscious emotions and thoughts. There are definite signs of you doing that here. You're honest, vulnerable...And the fact that you repeatedly fill spaces with nonsense like 'carrots and cheese' shows me that you aren't holding back. It's just naturally a little more organized than most. As you continue to work on these, you might find that you rely less on rhyming, or it may remain consistent. This is only your first try."

"We'll see what you have to say after I start compulsively rhyming in real life," I joke, feeling slightly better about item one on my checklist of concerns regarding the assignment.

"We both know how reluctant you've been to come back to Seattle to direct a show, and as we've discussed, your reasoning is completely valid. I still think it's a very big step for you to be returning to your hometown at all. You have every right to feel even more out of place than usual. Is there anything in particular you'd like to talk about before we move on?"

"There is one thing," I say, even though I could fill our whole hour with questions about the exercise. But ever since committing these words to digital paper, one section above all else is practically the only thing I have been able to think about. "Most of the stuff in there is, as you said, just a stream of consciousness. But I was kind of weirded out with how I ended it, saying I needed to Kill Beth."

Her thin eyebrows soften, and wrinkles form across her forehead. "People write all sorts of things during these sessions, just like we all sometimes have intrusive thoughts. I went grocery shopping the other day. On the way home, someone on the sidewalk bumped into me, and I dropped my bag and broke a glass bottle of kombucha. In the moment, I wished the guy would trip and fall into oncoming traffic. That doesn't mean I actually wanted him dead, nor does it mean I would ever actually push someone or anything like that. You know as well as anyone that sometimes we just have dark thoughts. Heck, if even half the people I talk to acted on flash thoughts or impulses, no one would make it a block in New York without killing someone. Though, I am curious as to who Beth is. I don't remember you mentioning her in any of our previous sessions. Who is she to you?"

I fake a laugh, but I don't know why. "That's just the thing. There's no one in my life named Beth. I don't think I even know an Elizabeth. It just came out."

"Is there anyone else right now that you're particularly upset with? Has anything happened since our Monday session that made you angry?"

I shake my head. "Just a smidge of resentment at Nate Mulligan for twisting my arm to take the job. Though, to be fair, I'm probably more angry at myself for saying yes."

Dr. Jules eases back, dropping any hint of concern. "In that case, it sounds like your mind was just grasping for a word that rhymes with *mess* and also expresses your discontent. It's just filler, like how you used 'carrots and cheese.'"

Her words make sense in my head, but there is a hitch in my chest. She is right, but I feel like I know something, which is going to bother me all day. I wouldn't be surprised to find myself digging through old playbills in the middle of the night, searching for any Beth I have worked with in the last few years, just to take the edge off this gnawing thought.

"Anything else?" she asks.

I tamp down my remaining hesitations about it, doing my best to force myself to move forward. Otherwise, I'll get hung up on this one detail for the rest of our hour, like a skipping record. "No, that's it for now."

She darts her eyes over to the side of the screen. Her mouse clicks when she closes the document. "All right, then. Keep at it, and we'll look at what you have for me in our next session. Tell me more about working with Nate again after all this time and how things are going with the cast."

My therapy session ends at 8:20, and rehearsal starts at 9:00. The Burgess Theater's rehearsal space is a fifteen-minute walk from Greenwood Terrace, with a five-minute extra allowance for pedestrian traffic.

While I walk, I click my teeth to the rhythm of my feet. It's a compulsion I catch myself engaging in whenever I am anxious or feel like my head is too full. I have numbered my teeth for musical notes, going from low to high. The left canine is one, left front tooth is two, two front teeth together are three, right front is four, and right canine is five. For the last few months, I have been consistently clicking my teeth to the baseline of the White Stripes's song "Seven Nation Army." With my footsteps as a consistent drum, I clatter out the droning melody in my skull.

One, one, five, four, three, two, one. Repeat ad nauseam until my jaw hurts.

The rehearsal basement is a multi-room area under the Odante Museum in Seattle's arts district. I do not trust elevators and instead prefer to take the four sets of stairs, which follow a square pattern down to the space. To end each flight properly, I follow a step pattern of odd, even, even, odd. Although I would prefer for all flights of stairs to be even numbered, I appreciate that there is at least a pattern in how the flights go about their asymmetry.

Because the space is so far underground, there are no windows. Without the heat and lights on, it can feel like spelunking into a deep cavern. Thankfully, the only person even more punctual than me is Burgess's in-house stage manager, Eden Michaels, who always has the power on by the time I arrive.

I love stage managers, and for the most part, stage managers love me. This is because their job description is eerily similar to my natural compulsion for preparation. Eden keeps the crew hitting their target dates for set building, costumes, sound, and lighting. She manages the talent scheduling, allowing me to focus on the creative decisions and work on getting the best performances out of my actors.

There is never a shortage of work-related talk for us to engage in, so I don't have to worry about idle chit-chat in regard to her outside life, friends, or family. Conversely, I don't have to ever mention the complete and total absence of all those things in mine. At the end of the day, we congratulate each other for our hard work, say goodbye, and then don't have to speak again until the next morning, when we will have a litany of new show-related issues to discuss.

Eden is a Black woman in her mid-thirties, with a round face and intense blue eyes that always demonstrate laser focus. She keeps her hair short and practical, just like me. Her work wardrobe is almost entirely made up of black clothing, which isn't uncommon for crew in the world of theater—yet another small comfort, something I can depend on every time I see her.

I appreciate Eden for many reasons, but most of all, we get along well because I can genuinely say I like her without having to worry about us ever being labeled as friends.

We are no more than five minutes into discussing upcoming costume fittings when the show's playwright, Nate Mulligan, hustles in. Unlike Eden, Nate is a social butterfly and loves to chat about anything and everything. We have known each other for nearly twenty years; both of us got our start working in this very theater. In my youth, I would have considered him my best friend. And since I don't really have any others, I guess I still do.

Even though we had not spoken to each other in nearly fifteen years, he called me one day, out of the blue, several months ago, begging me to come direct his newest play in the place I landed my first ever directing gig. Despite our shared trauma over what happened during that production, he somehow convinced me to say yes. And so, here I am, in the hometown I haven't visited since my twenties.

"Good morning, everyone. How are we all doing today?" He approaches from behind and gives me an exuberant squeeze on the shoulder.

"I'm going to run to the restroom before we get started." Eden excuses herself from the table before Nate gets a chance to chat her up.

"Mike, how's the head shrink? Everything good?"

I regret mentioning to Nate about meeting with my therapist on Friday mornings. It feels weird that he would remember such a detail, and I don't think it is appropriate to discuss my mental health in so casual a manner. But this is the way of Nate, and I can't help but give him a pass.

"Still sane. At least for now. How are you?" Redirecting the conversation back onto him is my strategy when it comes to small talk. It works on almost everyone, and I would say it's about seventy percent effective with Nate. Unfortunately, this is not one of those times.

"You warming back up to Seattle? It's not so bad once you're settled in, right?"

"Sure."

But I hesitate a fraction of a second, and Nate catches it. He narrows his eyes.

"You know what you need? A good meal. I'm taking you out tonight after rehearsal. My treat."

I open my mouth to protest, but he beats me to it.

"I know you have nothing else going on. Come on. We can even bring the script with us if you want and call it a working dinner."

Outside the rehearsal room, an elevator dings. The actors are here.

Shakespeare's Head Pub stands as a monument to the arts district, one of our main haunts back when we were twenty-somethings. The exterior of the old bar and grill looks almost the same amidst a sea of unfamiliar buildings. It is on the second floor, above a gelato shop which used to be a Mexican restaurant. I can still remember the odd number of stairs leading to the entrance of the pub, even after all these years.

Aside from an upgraded karaoke setup and some flat-screen TVs, the place is exactly as I remember it. I would wager money there is still a sign over the urinal which reads: "We aim to please, so you aim too, please."

Nate leads me to a corner table. The sign says to wait for a hostess, but I assume he has remained a regular customer, enough to feel like the standard rules don't apply to him. Sure enough, a waitress immediately greets us with a big smile.

"What can I get started for ya?" she asks with a pen and paper in hand.

"Club soda and lime," I say.

"Make it two," Nate agrees.

Once she's gone, Nate leans back and soaks in the atmosphere. "Just like the good old days, huh?" He smiles, but there is a tiredness to his eyes.

Also, the fact neither of us is drinking in the English pub stands out as notably different from said "old days." In our earlier lives, we would get started on shots the moment we sat down, and by the end of the night, we would be so tanked I wouldn't even remember getting back home half the time. But all that is long behind us. I have no idea how well he has stuck to the pact we made sitting on the steps of Greenwood Terrace fifteen years ago, but I haven't had a single drink since.

Nate is fit for his forties, without even a single gray strand mixed in with his black hair and meticulously groomed beard. One time, an actor's kid said to him, "You look like a bad guy, but I know you're a good guy." It was the most perfect and succinct summation of Nate I had ever heard.

"So, be honest with me, Mike. How are you doing? No bullshit."

The words twist in my heart. I want to start clicking my teeth but need to use my mouth to provide an answer. "I knew it would be hard coming back here," I say.

"And..."

"In some ways, it's even harder than I thought. You know I still have nightmares about the apartments, the theater. About that night. I was hoping that coming back would feel different, but it doesn't."

"Shit, man. You're making me feel guilty for asking you to come."

My drink is set in front of me, and I pause for a moment to collect my thoughts while I take a sip. "My therapist thinks this is a good opportunity for growth. Facing my past and all that." I don't know what else to say, so I stare down at my club soda and drink more.

Nate's face falls slightly. "Screw it. Let's not talk about depressing shit. I didn't mean to drum up bad times. Why don't we get down to business?"

Some of my favorite words. "Yes, please."

"You should start by telling me again how great my script is."

As silly as his begging for praise is, at least it is a chance to be fully honest and back in my comfort zone. "You know it's fantastic. No offense to you, but there isn't a snowball's chance in hell I'd be back in Seattle if it wasn't one of the best scripts I've ever gotten to work with."

Nate beams. "You know I named it after you, right?"

"Yeah, I got that."

The play is called *Wherever You Go*, a shorthand for the phrase, "Wherever you go, there you are." I used to say that all the time back when I was starting out. Between school, internships, and working my way up to that first director's job, I had been a constant traveler from the moment I graduated high school. Back then, I used to mean it in a positive sense; it was almost a mantra of self-sufficiency. All I needed was my suitcase and a beer and it didn't matter where I was. The world was my stage—to borrow another apt phrase.

Now it has taken on a completely different meaning. These days, "Wherever you go, there you are" means my guilt, anxiety, and constant fear are stuck to me like sap. No matter where I am around the country, no matter the show I'm working or the people I surrounded myself with, there I am: a person whose fuck-up has dictated every facet of his existence for his entire adult life.

The play reflects the sentiment beautifully, though the events are totally different from our lives. It centers around a married couple on the verge of divorce after a miscarriage and a husband's subsequent affair with his boss. The couple move from the city to the country, believing a change of scenery will help reset their marriage. But, of course, it is never that simple.

While things start out on the right foot, older, deeper-rooted issues and patterns start to emerge, and they are forced to realize they can't outrun their problems. The story culminates in a hurricane which nearly destroys the couple's home and ends with them the morning after, wondering aloud if it is possible to rebuild.

The script really struck a chord with me, from beginning to its poignant and ambiguous ending. If it had been presented to me literally anywhere else, I would have clawed to get my hands on it. Instead, I had Nate shoving it at me, practically on his knees to have me take it on.

Even though we had not stayed in touch for nearly two decades, it was as if Nate had climbed into my head and my heart and typed out two acts of pure catharsis, if that is something I am even capable of experiencing anymore. But the one thing I did know, without a doubt, was that I could do this project. I could bury myself in the script and feel proud of the work I had done bringing it to the stage. And somehow, Nate knew that too.

I want to share this with him, to tell him he reached into my soul and plucked out the perfect story, but vulnerability is a use-it-or-lose-it skill, and I lost it years ago.

Instead, I just nod my head and sip more of my club soda and lime.

The waitress returns to take our orders, but before I can ask for an old-fashioned fish and chips, an eruption of excitement behind me draws my attention. Four people enter the pub: Cassandra Mollie, Alexander Keating, Elaine Estabrook, and Danny Sparks. The entire cast of our play.

"Hey!" they shout, hurrying to our table, calling things like "Small world" and "What a coincidence!"

Nate stands up to say hello to everyone.

Meanwhile, I feel like a teacher who has just gotten caught by one of their students while pursuing the aisles of a sex toy shop. Heat blasts from my cheeks; embarrassment dresses me up and down like a three-piece suit. My shirt's collar is suddenly too tight, and I pull at it to keep from choking. The cast approaches, and my teeth click.

One, one, five, four, three, two, one. "Seven Nation Army."

"Hey, everyone," I manage to say, doing my best to keep from flinching when they come in for cordial hugs.

"Would you like a bigger table to sit together?" the waitress asks.

"Absolutely," Danny says.

Nate agrees. "The more the merrier."

"Actually, I'm just heading out." I conjure an excuse to get out of casual fraternization. "Need to get some prep work done for tomorrow."

"Seriously?" says Cassandra, the female lead known simply as Wife in the script. "Stay for a drink!"

"I can't, sorry. Wish I could." *I've got some oven knobs to count back at my apartment. If I don't, the whole place might burn down.* "Don't stay out too late. We're starting costume fittings tomorrow, and we'll be blocking from Act 1, Scene 5!"

I forget to say goodbye to Nate. Don't even look at him while I scramble out of the pub. I try to loosen a tie which isn't there. Unable to breathe. This place is bad for me; this pub is bad for me. It's where everything started, and I can't let that happen again.

Once outside, I gasp for breath like a deep-sea swimmer who just set a record. I am so frazzled I nearly forget to take the first step of the staircase down. The last thing I need right now is to follow the wrong pattern. If I did, I would have to go all the way back up and down again properly, and I'm already embarrassed enough.

The winter air cools me down while I make my way back to Greenwood Terrace. The whole time, my teeth click to the White Stripes. My heartbeat is just about back to normal when I notice movement in the alley behind the building.

A stranger rummages through the dumpster. His hair and beard are long and scraggly. He is dressed in at least four layers of jackets and shirts. A shopping cart nearby is full of clothes, cardboard, and blankets.

"Kill Beth!" he shouts with slurring words, catching me staring at him.

"What did you say?" I ask, nearly bowled over in shock.

"I said, what the hell you looking at?" He takes a step toward me, and that familiar heat returns to my face.

"Before that, you said...I...Never mind." Even though my face is hot, my hands shake. I make my way to my apartment and fumble the key against the door.

Once inside, I pace the single room, rubbing my hands up and down my face, trying to simultaneously warm up and cool down. I couldn't have heard him right.

Even though I try to do my breathing exercises Dr. Jules taught me, I'm too agitated. I don't know what else to do, so I sit down, open my laptop, and start typing.

Spontaneous Writing: Session 2

What are you looking at? What are you looking at?
Under attack
no taking it back,
Carrots and cheese, whats wrong with me
you dont want to be here
you DO NOT want to be here
Set up by Nate, Set up by fate
Its all too much to have on your plate
Kill Beth, thats what he said
you swear you heard it, swear on your death
Kill Beth, at Shakespeares Head
Cut off her hands, chop off her feet
Slit the throat, cook the meat
Cut the mesh, break on in,
Make sure her things aren't seen again
Throw the parts into the sea
When theres nothing left of her, you're free
Wherever you go, there you are
You've come too close, you've gone too far
Now they all think you're a freak

Theres nowhere to hide, not under your sheets
Not in your bed
where Beth is dead
Ambushed by cast, you werent prepared
Theres nothing to fear, no need to be scared
You see them every day, its true,
But do they, can they, ever see you?
You shouldn't have gone out with Nate
Remember your mantra, isolate.
Meetings for work, not meetings with friends
Impossible to make amends
Don't listen to Nate, he won't understand
He lives in the world, with the everyday man
He drinks non-drinks down at the pub
He's everyone's friend, he's everyone's bud
He's not like you, He's totally free,
Carrots and cheese, carrots and cheese.

Chapter 2

I'm late. This never happens, and it fills me with anxiety while I rush to rehearsal. For whatever reason, my alarm didn't go off this morning. I pass all the other dark and silent apartments; the cast left before me. My teeth click in time with every running step to work.

My hand quakes when I open the door to the rehearsal space. It reminds me of when I sat down last night for my spontaneous writing session. I had hoped it would calm me down, but by the time I was done, my whole body was shaking uncontrollably. A shower was necessary just to get my muscles to stop twitching.

I spent hours in bed, staring at the ceiling, coming up with ways I could have misheard him. The closest I got was "filled mess"? Like maybe the dumpster was overly full? The more I tried to do mental gymnastics to come up with something else, the more indelible the words became, chiseled in my brain.

When I woke up this morning, I swear I was actually sore from shaking so hard. It was as if my body had invented a new type of anxiety-based workout. I couldn't get the vagrant's words out of my head. The same ones I had typed. I was sure he had said, "Kill Beth."

Kill Beth.

My tension eases once I spot Eden sitting in her chair, ready to work. She has a yellow notepad, a page already filled with items to review. It pulls me out of my head and gives me something new and important to focus on. Not to mention, the actors are all there, ready for rehearsal.

We get straight to work, blocking out one of the more tense scenes in Act One running up to the inciting incident. After Wife has her miscarriage, Husband shuts down emotionally and refuses to talk to her about anything serious. Attempting to connect, Wife brings a home-made lunch to Husband at work, only to nearly catch him cheating with The Boss. This plants the seed of doubt into Wife's head and calls back to an earlier part of the play, where she thinks she smells perfume on Husband's shirt. It is a scene full of nuance and subtlety which will lead to the explosive argument in Scene 7, where Wife confronts him.

Nate slips in a half hour later than me and silently grabs a seat at the table. I am relieved to not have to talk with him, still so embarrassed over how I left last night. The cast doesn't know me outside of work mode and hopefully just sees me as a slightly eccentric but otherwise normal director.

Keeping isolated from the cast outside of rehearsal is not only allowed; it's often encouraged. There is a litany of reasons, many of which are similar to why an office manager isn't friends with their employees. There needs to be a line, one clearly defined between the visionary and their instruments to maintain a position of respect and stay clear from interpersonal drama or perceived favoritism. The director has to put themselves above the relationships and camaraderie which form amongst the cast.

Finally, there has to be a level of trust that the director knows what is best for the production at all times. If I'm out drinking with the actors and showing them my true self, they might realize what an absolute mess of a human being I am. How can they trust a captain to guide them when their captain is barely holding himself together?

I'm aware this is not the strategy for every director. But I am *not* every director. I'm me. And I can't allow myself to get close to these people.

Not again.

Nate, on the other hand, is a completely different story. He and I have history. Nate witnessed me panic yesterday and will assuredly confront me about it later.

Sure enough, when we break for lunch, he practically jumps out of his chair and pulls me aside before I can sneak away.

"Hey, Mike, can we talk?"

"Sorry. I have to get to costumes. We're starting fittings this afternoon and—"

"Come on. Be real with me. What happened last night?"

I shake my head, unbelieving. He is trying to make me talk about it when he probably knows damn well what happened. Instead of answering, I go on the offensive.

"Why don't *you* tell me? Did you have that little ambush planned or what?"

"Ambush? Are you kidding?"

"No, I'm not kidding. Did you invite the cast to join us without telling me?"

Nate rears back, either feigning or in genuine shock. "Of course I didn't. Why would I? What possible reason would I have to put together a shindig for you without looping you in?"

I'm dangerously close to raising my voice, with the cast just a few feet away. Some of my gusto is lost when I am forced to open and close the fridge in the common area before leading Nate over to Rehearsal Room B. I shut the thick soundproof door behind us.

"I don't know what you want from me, Nate. You call me out of the blue, ask me to come back here when you know I've spent almost two decades actively avoiding The Burgess Theater. Then you ask me to grab some dinner and take me to, of all places, Shakespeare's Head. You tell me about how I'm the inspiration to your story. You want to talk about how I'm doing, how the story's affecting me...all this personal shit. Then all of a sudden, here comes the cast, looking like they're ready to party."

"No one was partying, Mike. They were just getting together for a couple after-work drinks and dinner. It's what normal people do to get to know each other better."

"Well, I'm *not* a normal person," I say. "I don't know what's going through your head. I'm not a mind reader. So yeah, I'm questioning if you called them to stage some sort of backdoor icebreaker. I don't know who you are now. It's been fifteen years since we've spoken. I mean, Christ, are you even still sober?"

"Hey, fuck you!" Nate shouts. "I've been nothing but good to you, Mike. And you keep acting like I'm running some sort of devious plot to do what, exactly? Get you to loosen up a little? Fuck me, right? No, I haven't had a drink in years. And no, I had no idea anyone was coming to the pub last night. You want to know *why* I invited you there? Because it's my favorite spot. I know we have bad memories there, and I'm sorry you took off and never processed your shit, but I'm still tethered here. I've learned to deal with my problems so I don't have a fucking panic attack when I walk into the same pub I eat at three times a week.

"And you know *why* the cast was there? Because they're fucking actors, and it's a bar and restaurant with cheap drinks and in the middle of the goddamn arts district! You think there needs to be a top-secret plan in order for stage actors to go to a place named after Shakespeare? Get your head out of your ass.

"And since you're so desperate for the truth right now, you want to know why else I go to Shakespeare's Head? Why I still live here and work at The Burgess? Because the truth is, what happened wasn't your fault. It wasn't *either* of our faults. We were young and dumb. It could have happened to anyone."

I shake my head. "But it *didn't* happen to anyone. It happened because of me. *I* did it. I was responsible. She trusted *me* to lead her, to take care of her, and I failed, and she died."

There is a knock at the door. Terror streaks up my body that we were being too loud. That the cast all heard every word we said. That my history is going to get out and the trust they have been putting into me will vanish.

Eden enters, wearing a look of concern. Never a good sign for an unflappable stage manager.

"Mike, I just got a call from maintenance. There's been a break-in at Greenwood Terrace."

We take a recess from rehearsal, and the seven of us rush over to the apartments. On the first floor, a huge slash has been made in the mesh covering an open window to 1B—Alexander Keating's apartment, our lead actor playing the role of Husband.

"Oh my god." Alexander lifts his scrawny arms and runs his fingers through his long, dark hair. He pulls keys from his pocket, but the door is unlocked.

The room has been ransacked. Drawers have been ripped from their dressers and tossed on the floor. Clothes are strewn about. Alex is searching wildly around a desk table he moved from his back nook over to the front window.

"No, no, no, no, no, no! They stole my laptop!"

"Let's all calm down. Everyone look around. Where did you have it last?" Eden asks.

"Right here!" Alex points to a spot on the desk directly below the gash in the window's mesh.

Danny Sparks, the actor who plays Wife's Brother/Doctor/Neighbor, hisses inward through his teeth. "Ooooh," he coos, like he is watching a bride trip and fall on her way up to the altar. "You just left it right in the open? In a street-facing ground-floor apartment?"

"I mean…it was shut, and so was the window," Alex says.

Danny winces out of embarrassment. "Yeah, but, like, did you lock the window?"

"Yes…I think so." Alex starts pacing, searching the same obvious empty spots over and over.

Danny fingers the latch on the window. "It doesn't feel like you locked it."

Alex starts to hyperventilate. "That had all my important pictures on it. My dad, my brother…Everything important was on that computer!"

Last year, Alex's brother, Landon Keating, died from a stunt gone wrong on a horror-themed reality game show called *Slashtag*. Several years before that, his father, legendary actor Great Scott Keating, died of old age. While Great Scott was world-renowned for both film and highly acclaimed Shakespeare performances, I was only passingly familiar with Landon, who was mostly known for some schlocky horror movie where he played a serial killer.

Unlike his movie star relatives, Alex has stuck to the stage.

That said, he also isn't the brightest bulb in the pack. It has been clear to me from day one that Alex comes from a place of ultra-privilege, and while he doesn't seem to have the pretentious air of his brother or father, he clearly has some gaps when it comes to common sense.

"Why would you put your laptop here, where anyone walking along the sidewalk could see it?" Danny asks, almost egging him on.

"I like to have a nice view when I'm working!" Alex says, as if it were the most obvious thing in the world.

Eden, ever the problem solver, steps in. "Listen, it's not your fault. We've unfortunately had break-ins here before. You had a MacBook, right?"

"Yeah," Alex says.

"Then you probably have everything backed up on the cloud, don't you?"

Alex takes a few deep breaths, then seems to calm a little. "Oh. Yeah."

"So, nothing's lost that can't be replaced. We'll have our company manager drive you to the Apple store this afternoon and get you a new one. Maybe after that, I'd suggest moving your desk and storing your valuables out of sight when you're not here."

Alex nods. "Okay."

When I eventually climb back up to my apartment, I am shocked to find my door is unlocked as well. Before I think to shout out to Eden, I look inside.

Nothing has been taken.

After touching the burner knobs and fridge door, I meticulously search every drawer, every nook and cranny, for any signs of entry, all the while clicking my teeth.

One, one, five, four, three, two, one.

Nothing is gone. Nothing out of place.

Just when I'm starting to think I must have just forgotten to lock my door this morning, I see it.

Something has been moved—or rather *removed*—from my trash can.

I'm sure I threw away my printed page of spontaneous writing after yesterday's session with Dr. Jules. And yet, I find it sitting on my laptop.

Spontaneous Writing: Session 3

Isolation Isolation
Keep your distance, know your station
These people are not your friends
You can never make amends
Nate is not your friend
Eden is not your friend
Beth is not your friend
But if you kill her your problems will end
Nothings wrong with feeling sorrow
Loneliness cannot be borrowed
Being alone is not so sad
You have yourself, that's not too bad
Sadness wraps you in a sheet
Keeps you warm, keeps you neat
Revel in sadness, make it your own
Make that feeling like a home
Carrots and cheese, sugar and snaps
Keep your heart behind the glass
Watch the flame burn from afar
Get too close and watch it char

Smash the glass, and take the shards,
Shove them in Beth's face and arms
Carve into her flesh and see
The glass is not for your safety
It's a weapon, crystal sharp
Slit her throat while in the dark
Drive the glass into her heart
Watch her drain out, thats a start
Dig in crystals by the dozen
It's easy when it's done with loving
Track Beth down, take it away
Make her suffer, make her pay
I know all the things she's done
So tie her up and start the fun
Do it for us, we'll even help
Do it for us, send Beth to hell

Chapter 3

While the rehearsal rooms are thick and soundproof, the walls and floors of Greenwood Terrace are paper-thin. Usually, management puts me up in a separate complex or in a hotel room for the duration of my jobs. The theater's owner, Rebecca Burgess, already owned these apartments when she opened the theater, which she donated to her business for her temporary employees. But thanks to her generosity, I am stuck in extremely close quarters with the cast.

Danny sings Taylor Swift while he gets ready in the morning on the first floor. I know when Elaine, the eldest cast member playing the roles of Husband's Boss/Neighbor, is having a smoke break, not just from the smell, but because I can hear every word of her phone conversation with her husband and son back in Los Angeles.

Their lives permeate into my room by osmosis. It's inescapable and gets in the way of my routine. I am not supposed to see any cast members in the morning or after rehearsal. But here, they are an ever-present source of noise and distraction.

Tonight, there is shouting so loud it jolts me from my already lousy sleep.

Before bed, I was on a marathon of clicking my teeth, checking and re-checking every inch of my apartment for signs of disturbance, after discovering the paper on my computer. If I were less anxious, I would probably be able to remember clearly whether I threw it away or had the intent.

Despite seeming like an insane thing to do, I haven't been able to stop hyper-fixating on the idea that someone has been in my apartment. To what end, though, I have no idea.

I check my phone: 3:14 a.m.

My first thought is that Alex and Cassandra are rehearsing one of the more heated arguments from the play. We finished blocking Act 1 earlier today. Maybe they are having a late-night pickup session?

But that doesn't make sense. Tomorrow is Monday—our one day off per week. Tonight and tomorrow night are generally the two times everyone, cast and crew included, tries to distance themselves from the work which otherwise swallows every aspect of their lives.

I sit up and try to click on the bedside lamp.

It's one of those lamps with the rotating knob that inexplicably requires you to click it twice before the light turns on. The knob itself is bent, which drives me a little crazy. It feels wrong to have the light click on while the knob is in the downward position. Practically every light switch I have ever used tells me down means *off*. I end up turning it on and off several times until the light comes on while the knob is pointing slightly upward.

Once I really start to listen, a cascade of new concerns trickle down in rapid succession.

First, the voices don't sound like Alex and Cassandra. It's definitely a man and a woman, but a third voice occasionally chimes in too—a young boy caught in the crossfire. I start to wonder if Elaine's family has journeyed up from California to visit her. Perhaps they are having some sort of disagreement.

But that doesn't quite feel right either.

The voices don't sound like they are coming from below me. Instead, they seem to be in the room next door, apartment 3B. But that is not possible. I'm the only one staying on the third floor.

Rubbing my eyes shakes any last traces of grogginess out of me.

Each apartment is outfitted with a small fireplace. Maybe the sound is being carried up the chute and is playing tricks on my ears. I try to listen more intently to what they are shouting about but can only make out bits and pieces.

"I don't care what you say. I don't want you spending time with that girl, do you understand me?" the woman scolds.

"You're overreacting. It's not a big deal!" a boy squeals, on the verge of throwing a tantrum.

"I had...all the time when I was..." The man's voice doesn't resonate as well through the wall. It's hard to pin down what he is saying.

"What am I supposed to do all day? I'm bored!" The kid's words all string together into one long whine.

I don't know what to do. My mind starts to race with ideas.

Could these be squatters? Did Elaine move? Did the theater already bring in new actors to start rehearsing for the next show? Most importantly, why is this all happening in the middle of the night?

Any irritation from being woken up is replaced by curiosity and just a touch of nervousness. One reason I enjoy my solitude is because I don't have to wonder about other people's lives intersecting with mine. I can experience the world on my terms. But whether I like it or not, I am part of this now.

A voice in my head tells me to leave it alone, but at the same time, a drum beating in my chest warns me it won't quit until I investigate this further. Maybe if I head out onto the balcony, I can hear them more clearly. Or better yet, if I work up the nerve, maybe I could knock on their door and politely inform them they are broadcasting their fight across the entire building.

It only takes a few seconds to climb out of bed and throw some pants on, but before I can make it even halfway across the room, I stop dead in my tracks. Prickles of fear tingle across my head and down my spine.

Through the thin cream-colored curtains of my window, the silhouette of a person walks past my apartment, headed from the stairs on the right toward the apartment on my left. A second later, he paces back the other way.

There is no emotion in his movement, no indications of stress or anger. From what I can tell by the shadow, they are just calmly walking back and forth, arms at their sides.

And they don't stop.

I count four, five, six times the shape passes my room. The footsteps are heavy enough to come from a man, loud enough I can hear them over the argument next door. I focus on the sound. He doesn't seem to venture down the entire walkway or even past the arguing couple's apartment.

The figure is only pacing in front of my unit.

The shape moves far enough past my window to a place where I can't see him, pivots, then comes back the other way. He does this again, and again, and again. I have lost count.

Tingling fear manifests itself in my hands and knees.

A shiver runs through my body when I remember the vagrant who yelled at me from the alley, the break-in at Alex's apartment, and my suspicion that someone had been in mine. What if it's the same person? What could he want from me? The bedside light I turned on clearly makes it visible to the man outside that I am in here and awake. So, he must know he is messing with me. The question is why?

I grab my cell phone and type in 911, keeping my finger hovered above the call button while I slowly approach. The thought of opening my curtains is too nerve-wracking, but there is a peephole on the door.

A quick glance around my apartment yields no results for any sort of practical weapon to defend myself. Even if I had a baseball bat, I would have no idea how to use it effectively. I haven't swung a bat since I convinced my mother to let me quit all sports when I was nine.

It takes several deep breaths to work up the nerve to inch forward again, and my fear doubles when the pacing figure seems to pick up speed the closer I get. I'm on my tiptoes, thankful my footfalls are silenced by a carpet. After several more breaths to psych myself up, I press my face against the door and stare through the distorted fishbowl lens.

There is no one outside.

I try to angle my head to the right to see over further, but it does no good. When I pull away from the door, a silence falls over the apartment, like a vacuum sucking all the air out of the room.

No more shouting from next door. No more shadow pacing in front of my apartment.

Absolutely nothing.

Somehow, that scares me even more.

A compulsion comes over me. I can't bear the question of it, so I flip the lock and rip my door open.

In the apartment next to me, all the lights are off. I peer over the rail, but there are no shapes rushing down the stairs. No one is scurrying back to another unit.

For the first time in a long time, I wish there was someone in my life I wasn't paying to talk to. Someone I could call at three in the morning, who could calm me down or even just listen. I scroll through my phone and glance at Nate's name for a second before scoffing at the idea and closing my contacts app.

When I get back inside my room, I lock the door and check the oven and fridge to keep myself safe.

Morning cannot come soon enough. While I am sure I managed to catch another couple of hours of sleep, I'm not aware of it. By the time my alarm goes off, I'm more than ready to start my routine. Thankfully, I have my Monday meeting with Dr. Jules and can't wait to get into it.

"I've got two sessions of spontaneous writing for you," I say before she even greets me.

"And how are they going?" she asks.

"I don't know if I'm doing them right. Some stuff makes sense, but there's other parts that are just weird. And not just carrots-and-cheese type of weird."

Her eyes shift over to her inbox, and she opens the first of the two documents.

"One thing I'm noticing is that you're writing these all in second person. You almost always seem to refer to yourself as 'you' instead of 'me,'" she says. "Why do you think that is?"

I shake my head. Honestly, this is the first time I have noticed it. "I have no idea. That's just how it comes out. Is there something wrong with that?"

"Not at all. Just curious, as it's somewhat unusual for people to journal outside of first person. I see Beth makes quite the reappearance."

I let out a deep breath. "It's weird to say this, but I feel like it's not even me writing about her. It just sort of shows up there on the page, in between the parts that I am writing."

Dr. Jules smiles and nods in affirmation, like she's proud of the gruesome details I've subconsciously spat into the document.

"That's exactly what we want to see with spontaneous writing. It's not just a journaling of your consciousness; you're supposed to let your mind drift off and let your hands take over to bring out latent feelings in unexpected ways. If you wrote everything with forethought and intention, it wouldn't be very spontaneous, would it?"

I try to stir up a smile through my exhaustion. "Yeah, I guess you're right."

"I'm seeing one part here that's quite interesting. What do you think you mean when you say 'Cut the mesh, break on in?'"

I read back the section of my document to refresh my memory. "Oh, you know. One of the actors had his apartment broken into. He got robbed, and the burglar gained access by cutting the screen to the window."

"Well, that explains a lot of the angst in some of your writing here. You're processing the trauma from that incident."

I scrunch my eyebrows and look back at the date on the doc. Fresh anxiety brings me to full attention.

"Actually, now that I think about it, I wrote that *before* the break-in." My restless leg instantly goes into overdrive, so much so that my whole chair starts to vibrate. How could I possibly write something so specific before it happened?

"Mike, remember…These don't all have to make sense or fit into any real events. You, in particular, have a strong tendency to search for associations and patterns where there are none. Speaking of, I see you've kept the rhyme scheme pretty consistent."

I shrug. "I don't know. It just seems to help."

"You also mention Nate quite a bit in this, saying he ambushed you. Do you want to talk about that at all?"

I shake my head. "I was being stupid. It's exactly like you're saying. I think I was searching for meaning and patterns. I agreed to go out with him to grab dinner last Friday, and the cast showed up randomly. I had a panic attack and left."

"You know that it's all right to have a meal with your castmates, right? I understand that you have your reasons to not become best friends with any of them, but that doesn't mean you can't be cordial."

"I just wasn't prepared. You know how I like to have a structure for my social interactions...or at least get the time to prepare properly. If there's a purpose to the conversation, I'm fine. It's when the goal is pure socialization that I freeze up."

Dr. Jules types something and shakes her head. "Mike, I'm reading your next entry. The whole first half of it is centered around trying to justify isolating yourself. What did we say about self-isolation?"

"That it's the best way to avoid conflict?" I show her a few too many teeth in a big phony grin.

"That no man is an island. I know you talk to people all day for work, and that's wonderful. But it's not going to kill you if you get to know someone a little bit. Having a conversation here and there about the weather or someone's family or friends is very different from what happened before. You understand that, right?"

"Yeah," I say, mostly to appease her. "I just feel like it can be a really slippery slope. You have one conversation about your favorite food, and the next thing you know, you're...Everything has gone to hell."

"I promise it doesn't work that way. For one thing, you're a very different person now than you were fifteen years ago. If you weren't, Rebecca Burgess wouldn't have had you back at her theater, would she?"

"Probably not." I feel like a kid being scolded by a teacher.

"You don't drink; you don't do drugs. You've driven yourself so far in the opposite direction that I can't imagine you falling into any of the same traps as before. Today is a day off for you, correct?"

I nod. "Yeah."

"And what do you have planned?"

I try to cook up an answer as fast as I can, but my life is so boring I can't even think of a single thing normal people do with their free time. "I don't know. Read a book? Prep for next week? Kill someone named Beth?"

Dr. Jules smirks. "What about your actors? What about Nate? What are they doing today?"

I consider withholding information, but I'm a terrible liar. Much like Nate, Dr. Jules seems to have an ability to sniff out deception from a mile away.

"It's actually Danny Sparks's birthday. He's one of the cast members. They're all having a barbecue down in the common area of the complex tonight."

"And were you invited?"

I sigh. "Yeah."

"Then that's your homework. Go to the party. You don't have to stay all night, but have a hot dog, drink a soda. Get to know some of these people a little better."

"Fine."

"And do me a favor. After the party, sit down for another spontaneous writing session. I'm very curious to see what your mind produces from that experience."

I spend half the day trying to practice topics of conversation which don't have to do with the show and mostly come up empty: I don't watch much TV or movies, I don't listen to the same music as them, and I don't have any family. The more I think about how little we have in common outside of our profession, the more anxious I become.

Aside from a few obvious remarks about Seattle's drab winter weather, I don't really know what to talk about. Alex Keating's family has an interesting history, but they're all dead, so I don't want to mention that. Danny is primarily an actor in musicals. I guess I could wind him up on that and let him go, but I know next to nothing about Cassandra. Elaine has a husband and kid, but I haven't found out any more than that.

Nate has been notably absent from rehearsals since our blowout on Friday, but if he comes, I can try to make amends and hope he keeps things light. He always has something interesting to talk about. If nothing else, I can stand awkwardly just outside of an existing conversation—an upfront seat to watching the world pass me by.

It is as close to a game plan as I have, though what little I prepared to talk about flies right out of my head as soon as I hear lively chatter down in the common area. Stress pounds against my temples, almost as strong as during last night's unexplainable intrusion.

Laughter echoes up the building while I make my way down the stairs and onto the side patio. It's just the four actors enjoying food and drinks.

"Mike! I didn't think you were coming." Danny is wearing a glittery gold cardboard tiara, which almost matches his bleached blond hair, and a chef's apron that says: "Messy Bitch."

"Happy Birthday, Danny." I am carrying a meticulously wrapped box containing a Taylor Swift's Eras tour sweater inside. He sings her songs almost as compulsively as I count stairs, so I feel confident it will go over well.

"Aww, thanks, Mike. You didn't have to do that." He places it on an otherwise empty table.

No one else brought gifts. Immediately, I feel like a fish out of water.

I dig around through a cooler packed with ice and find a can of lime-flavored seltzer. Even though I don't drink alcohol, having something to sip on is a fantastic defense mechanism when I have nothing to say. If there is ever a lull in a conversation or I am awkwardly standing off to the side, I can just milk a long sip to appear busy. It's one of my favorite tricks.

Danny is in the middle of a story, and I have to keep my jaw from dropping while I listen.

"...So, anyway, me and Greg had never even heard of a fisting party, never mind going to one. But then we're like, 'Screw it; it's LA. Let's just go for the hell of it.' We walk in, and I shit you not, the whole house is coated in plastic sheeting. It's like a kill room from *Dexter* in there. And—I mean, I guess this is what we were there for, but still—right in the middle of the living room, there's a dude with his forearm halfway up this guy's asshole. And he's chugging along like a fucking steam engine and starts calling out to the dude, 'Hey, man, you need to relax. I see pink, I see pink! You need to relax!'"

"What does that even mean?" Cassandra asks, laughing so hard she is nearly crying.

"I guess it's a bad thing. I still don't really know, to be completely honest. But this dude wasn't going to stop, even though the other guy was clearly not having the time of his life. And, of course, as soon as someone tells you to relax, that's like the last thing you can possibly do. But sure enough, the guy that's doing the fisting just keeps repeating himself while choo-choo'ing like Thomas the fisting engine. 'I see pink! I see pink! You gotta relax, man!'"

"So what did you do?" Alex asks.

"We turned our pink asses around and got the hell out of there! Also, oh my god, I cannot even describe what it smelled like. I guess you don't really consider stuff like that before you find yourself in that particular situation. You think you know what ass smells like? I swear, you have no idea until you've been to a fisting party."

Danny continues to tell raunchy stories from his time in LA, and I chug down half of my sparkling water.

Out of nowhere, Elaine starts up a side conversation with me, clearly as gobsmacked by the story as I am.

"Well, that's a tale I didn't know I needed in my life. The last party I went to was for an eight-year-old. The most exciting thing I heard there was one of my son's friends telling me his favorite *Paw Patrol* characters ranked from best to worst. How about you? Any wild parties from the theater world?"

My mind immediately goes to the one party I have never told anyone about. Can't share that. But in a moment of almost shocking relief, I'm able to push past it and recall some tamer events I have been to over the course of my career.

Elaine is the only person here around my age. All the other actors are in their twenties. I try to think back to the most recent non-work function I attended, hoping I have something which might be interesting to share.

"My last party that was actually fun was a murder mystery." I leave out the fact it was almost seven years ago.

"Oh, that sounds so cool!"

"It was," I say and mean it. "You come in and get this little sheet of paper with your character and all this information, like blackmail on other people or details you're trying to gather. The thing I really loved about it was that it was a party with a purpose. So, if things ever got awkward, I always had a handy-dandy cheat sheet of topics to bring up. And any time you met somebody new, it was in the context of the game, which made it really easy."

"Ugh. I would love to do something like that. Anything with adults that doesn't include fisting and isn't an opening night party."

Again, I find a common point with her. "I know! I hate opening night parties. You'd think they would be for us, but it's all about the donors and season ticket holders."

"I swear, sometimes I feel like I'm doing more acting at those events than in the actual play. My face hurts by the end of the night from forcing myself to smile so much, and by the time I make it to the food station, all the good stuff's already picked clean."

"Does your family usually come to opening night?" I ask, realizing I have a path to asking about the argument I heard last night.

"Sometimes, if they're able."

"They aren't in town now, by any chance, are they?"

Elaine gives me a look that is hard to read. "No, why?"

I have already stuck my foot in it, so I might as well go the rest of the way. "I thought I heard a couple talking loudly last night, around three in the morning. And I could have sworn they had a kid with them. I'm sure you know by now how thin these walls are. I thought maybe your family might have come into town."

She shakes her head and gives me a slightly judging look for the insinuation. "You sure it wasn't someone on the street?"

I crook my mouth. It is a reasonable suggestion, but at the same time, I'm positive it was coming from the other side of my wall. "I don't think so. Maybe someone was just watching the TV too loud. You didn't hear anything at all?"

Elaine shakes her head. "Nope. But then again, with the amount of trazodone I take, I would probably sleep through the apocalypse."

Without a follow-up comment, I finish off my seltzer. "I'm going to grab another one of these. You want anything?"

She holds up a canned margarita. "I'm good."

I grab another seltzer from the cooler and give it a sip. To my surprise, I'm feeling pretty good, like I have just successfully navigated my way through a non-work-related adult conversation. Sure, it was short, and I may have mildly insulted her by accident, but if nothing else, I can bring this story to Dr. Jules as proof that I came down and did the assignment.

It isn't long before Danny finishes his next story and the floor opens to smaller conversations. Cassandra asks Elaine what it is like working while having a family, and I sort of join the conversation through proximity. But I don't feel awkward like I expected. Against all odds, I start having fun.

Our three-way conversation breaks off when the burgers Danny is grilling are ready, and as we sit down to eat, Alex asks me about some of the shows I have worked on in the past. It's the perfect question. I get to talk about work *without* talking about the work we're presently doing.

It turns out I have quite a few stories up my sleeve about shows gone wrong, bizarre actor behavior, and interesting encounters. I start to feel like they are really listening to me. And even better, they still respect me. At one point, I even have the whole table's attention while I tell them about an actress down in San Diego who found a spider on a chair in her room. Her response was to take every piece of furniture in the unit and pile it up on the balcony. This does not get quite the same response as Danny's fisting story, but that is okay with me.

By the time we have finished eating, the sun has sunk behind the buildings across the street, and a chill descends upon the patio. Danny asks if we all want to continue the party in his room. This is my opportunity—an easy way to tap out for the night. But I'm astonished when I agree to keep going. I pick up the cooler and carry it to Danny's apartment, pulling a third flavored seltzer out after I set it down in his kitchenette.

"Can we turn on the fire? I'm freezing," Cassandra says.

I volunteer, having used the one in my unit several times already. After sliding open the glass doors protecting the fireplace, I twist the gas knob, then place the lighter below the fake blocks of wood. The gas ignites, and just like that, we have a nice cozy fire going.

Conversations continue, and with each passing moment, more tension eases off. A connection is forming with this group. Maybe I have been too hard on myself for all these years. Perhaps there is a way to be friendly with my cast and still be a good director.

Nearly an hour passes, and there is no sign of things slowing down. Cassandra and I chat about the worst shows we have ever been attached to. She goes deep-sea fishing in the half-melted cooler, trying to find another drink.

"You want one?" she asks, finally pulling out a can.

"No, I don't drink," I say.

She squints at me, as if trying to tell if I am joking or not. "You sure about that?" She juts her chin at my seltzer.

At first, I don't understand...until I read the label more clearly. It is not *just* a flavored seltzer. It's a *hard* flavored seltzer. Meaning, it has booze.

"Oh shit," I say. The world twists on its axis. No wonder I have been so loosey goosey. I am three drinks in after a decade and a half of sobriety.

But I don't have long to ponder my fuck-up before Cassandra returns, her hand red and dripping from spending so much time fishing around the cooler. She shakes the ice water off, then drops to her knees in front of the fireplace.

"I need to warm up after that. My hand's as pink as the guy in Danny's story."

She reaches toward the fire.

Someone has slid the glass door shut in front of it. A crack in the glass starts to spiderweb across the pane.

"No! Wait!" I shout, but it's too late.

The differential of heat and cold on either side of the glass creates a small explosion. The entire door shatters outward, sending hundreds of shards rocketing at Cassandra. She screams so loud it becomes the only sound in the room. Her whole arm is embedded with glass.

But that is not the worst of it.

Her face is a collection of knicks and slashes, with over a dozen pieces of glass dug into her cheeks, jaw, and...

Oh God, her eye.

A shard, maybe an inch wide, has fully embedded into her right eye. I have no idea how deep it goes, but more than just blood is running down her face. A foamy yellowish-green fluid seeps from the socket.

"Call an ambulance!" Elaine shouts.

Danny lurches to his feet to grab his phone but trips over himself and vomits on the rug.

Cassandra's hand is shaking like a leaf. It slowly creeps toward the foreign object embedded in her eye. She barely touches it before letting out a shriek even louder than the first.

Elaine is talking to a dispatcher. Alex has a towel and is trying to figure out a way to wrap up Cassandra's arm, but there is too much glass. Nobody knows what to do.

It's an excruciating ten minutes of pure panic before flashing red lights and a siren pull up to the building. We are running around like chickens with their heads cut off while this woman wails on the floor, smearing blood all over the tan carpet. A pair of EMTs eventually hurry in, load her onto a stretcher, and rush her into the ambulance.

When the van drives away, we are left in a stunned silence.

Maybe it's the alcohol, but I feel like I need to fill the emptiness. "I tried to stop her when I noticed the glass."

"Who the fuck puts a glass door over a lit fire?" Danny shouts.

After another awkward silence, Danny pipes up again.

"That wasn't a rhetorical question. Who did it?"

"It wasn't me," Alex says, preemptively to his next statement. "But I had no idea you couldn't put glass over a lit fire. I certainly didn't think it would go off like that. Seems like a simple mistake."

"It doesn't matter." Elaine puts a hand on Danny's shoulder.

He jerks away, shrugging her off. "Yes, it fucking does! Who did it? Who lit the fire?"

I have a sudden urge to defend myself, even though nobody is looking at me. "I use the fireplace in my unit all the time," I say. "I was the one who noticed the door was shut when she reached out. There was a crack in it, and I thought maybe that could be why it was compromised so badly. I tried to stop her as soon as I noticed."

"Holy shit, this is so messed up!" Danny shouts.

I stand and back away to the door, pulling my phone from my pocket. "I'm sorry. I have to call Eden." Then I rush out of the room as fast as my legs will carry me.

In the aftermath of this horror, even with my inebriation, I don't fail to remember which steps to start on for every flight of stairs. By the time I reach my room, Eden is on the line.

"Something happened. Cassandra's hurt. She's going to the hospital," I say, hurrying over to the oven and fridge, tapping everything to help calm my nerves. I even turn the key to my fireplace to make sure it is off.

"What?" Eden says. "Slow down. What happened?"

"Someone closed the glass door on the fireplace. It had a crack, and it exploded. One of the shards...Oh god." I belch, fighting back burning acid and bile in my stomach while I am pulled back into the moment. The awful colors seeping from her popped eyeball are branded into my brain.

"Where are they taking her?" Eden asks.

"I don't know. They said the name. Give me a second." I get onto my computer to look up nearby hospitals, knowing I will recognize the name when I find it. But before I do, I see my last spontaneous writing session sitting on the screen. My eyes are immediately drawn to a passage:

Smash the glass, and take the shards

Shove them into Beth's face and arms

Carve into her flesh and see

The glass is not for your safety

It's a weapon, crystal sharp

Slit her throat while in the dark

Drive the glass into her heart

Watch her drain out, thats a start

. . .

First, the slashed mesh of the window. Now this. I wrote these words two days ago. It's too similar to be a coincidence.

I try to think back to when I lit the fire. I know better than to close the glass door over an open flame, even if it is supposed to be safe.

So I didn't do this, right?

"Eden, I'm going to have to call you back."

SPONTANEOUS WRITING: SESSION 4

Its all your fault, its all your fault
One night out and its falling apart
Youve said it once, youve said it again,
This is how it always ends
This is why you can't have friends
You've killed before, you know its true
Theres nothing else for you to do
You leave destruction in your wake
You cannot fix your own mistake
Theres only one path to escape
You must kill Beth to clean your plate
For what shes done to me, and more
Stick a knife into that whore
Gouge her eyes out, boil her brain
Run her over with a train
Deglove her hands
cut every strand
Rip out her teeth
So she cant screech
Its only right to do what's just

We need you to finish this job for us
Your soul is rotten, youre no good
Dig two graves out in the woods
One for you and one for Beth
The only cure for Mike is death
Carrots and cheese, carrots and cheese,
This is your fault, cant you see?
The only way to make it better
Is to go find Beth and then behead her.

Chapter 4

Tuesday's rehearsal is canceled, for obvious reasons. I am losing my mind. Part of me knows, down to my very core, that I did not slide the glass door over the fireplace. Not to mention, I specifically remember every other step of lighting the fire.

But who else would have touched it? *Why* would they?

But then I remind myself, whether I meant to or not, I *had* been drinking. I was acting out of character, not feeling myself. Could it have been a careless mistake?

Or something more sinister?

The more I take part in these spontaneous writing sessions, the less I feel in control. Dr. Jules said the whole point is to let go of myself when writing, but it is almost starting to feel like someone else is guiding my hands. I was not drinking when I forgot whether I threw away that paper from my spontaneous writing, and I'm still trying to figure that out.

Between the fire and the break-in at Alex's—and possibly my own apartment—I am starting to feel more sure that something is going on. And then, of course, there was the incident in the middle of the night, with the shouting neighbors and the pacing figure outside my room, which just seemed to vanish.

As much as I want to take a day off or run screaming for the hills altogether, there is a saying in theater that is as popular as it is for a reason.

The show must go on.

Eden and I head to the hospital first thing in the morning. She drives, and I couldn't be more grateful. In my current state, I don't know that I could drive a car without causing more calamity. My nerves are shot, and even after my morning latte, I still can't seem to scrub the heavy bags from under my eyes.

That is not even touching on the traces of a hangover. The pounding headache is almost as bad as the constant guilty reminder that I got drunk for the first time in ages. What is worse, I did it in front of the cast I have been actively working to build respect and trust with.

My mind can't stop spinning through events and conversations leading up to the incident. If I was drunkenly responsible for the glass and forgot, what other things could I have done that I don't remember? What embarrassing truths did I admit? What stories could I have told that would make them think less of me?

At one point, we were sharing horror stories from past productions. The honesty juice wiped out any ability for me to hold back. Are Alex, Danny, and Elaine thinking that I will be talking about this incident when I move on to my next project? How can they hold any trust or respect for me, knowing I will throw anyone under the bus for the sake of a good story?

This whole time, my teeth are tapping at ultra-speed, and there is nothing I can—or want—to do to slow them down. *One, one, five, four, three, two, one. One, one, five, four, three, two, four, two, one.*

And then there's Cassandra.

A nurse leads me and Eden into Cassandra's room, where her head and arms are completely wrapped up. One eye, a few holes for her nostrils, and a slit for her lips are all that is visible behind layers of bandages. Even with the amount of gauze and padding covering her other eye, there is still a vague circular stain of dried blood indicating the extent of her trauma.

Forget losing out on the role in the play—the woman lost her eye.

And all over something as stupid as trying to warm up her chilled hand in front of a fireplace.

"How are you feeling?" I ask, though I feel stupid for the question. But what else am I supposed to say to make this any less gut-wrenching of an experience? I am the captain of this ship, and I'm supposed to have the answers, inside and out of rehearsal. Instead, I'm just horrified, guilty, and completely lost.

"My mom's coming to see me," Cassandra mumbles. Her lips move slowly, her jaw tightly bound in her mummified face. The words are heavy and slurred under chemical sedation.

"When's she coming?" I hope that, by asking, I will somehow summon her to appear and give us a reason to get the hell out of here.

"Her flight gets in at...um...um...later. Later today. I can't wait to see her."

I open my mouth but have nothing to say. Thankfully, Eden comes to my rescue.

"Everyone at The Burgess sends their love and support. If you're up for it, the cast would like to come by and visit with you in a little while."

I have no idea if that is the truth or if providing comfort is just another skill in which Eden is a pro.

A strained smile drifts across Cassandra's mouth, if only for a second. "I'd like that. Sorry to ruin the party."

"Not at all," I jump in, smothering under the weight of my own perceived part in the accident and the shame which comes with it.

For as much as I will be punishing myself over this, Cassandra will probably re-live the events of last night every day for the rest of her life. She will have to learn to accept how something so simple, so innocuous, so casual, irreparably damaged her whole being.

While I don't have any physical scars to show it, I understand what it is like to live every day with regret over something that felt so small in the moment. At least with grand risks, we know the potential conse-quences and have a modicum of understanding that we only have ourselves to blame. But it's the regret and rage over the small moments which really haunt us because they feel so avoidable in hindsight.

A nurse walks in to check Cassandra's vitals and announces that the doctor is coming to run some tests. I hate to admit that I am relieved to have our visit cut short, but thankful we don't have to belabor our exit or make awkward small talk until we find some bullshit way to excuse ourselves from staring at this freshly broken woman any longer.

"I've already sent out sides to a number of local actresses," Eden says when we are back in the car. "It's all women we've worked with before, who come as close to Cassandra as I could think."

Normally, when a cast member drops out of a show this far into the rehearsal process, the easiest route is to promote an existing cast member from a smaller role, then recast *them* instead. But Elaine is too old for the part of Wife by a good ten years, at least.

Even though I barely got to know Cassandra as a person, she was excellent to work with. She carried the gravitas of a grieving mother-to-be and was adept at building her tension and showing her resentment until she exploded during multiple breaking points throughout their relationship. Even better, it was her chemistry read with Alex which had really clenched the role for her. They played off each other with such a level of intimate intuition one would have suspected they had worked together before this.

We don't have the luxury of a chemistry read this time around. Alex has been given the day off, and with two weeks until opening night, there isn't a moment to spare in getting our new lead actress cast and caught up. We should already be blocking the second act, but now we might need to spend several days retreading old ground. On top of that, I will need to work extra hours with our new lead to make up for lost time.

This show is already running on a tighter timeline than most productions I direct. As much as I hate to admit it, we simply don't have a day to waste.

As always, Eden is on top of her game to a degree that makes me wonder if she even sleeps. When she got word last night regarding the extent of Cassandra's injury, she sent out emails to actresses and scheduled four women to audition today at 3:00 p.m.

"You've personally worked with all these women before?" I ask, trying to keep myself present, only spiraling with worry about one thing at a time.

As harsh as it sounds, I must push off thoughts of last night, of

Cassandra's eye, and focus on the needs of the show. Right now, that means making sure these women are professional enough to handle the demands of a dramatic role such as this and the additional pressure of working under such special circumstances.

"Yes, Mike. I've worked with them all before, multiple times. They all know what they're potentially getting themselves into. It's going to be fine, I promise." Eden glances at me when we pull up to a red light. "You're doing a good job, Mike. This wasn't your fault."

I must be such a mess. Even at a casual glance, she can see right through me.

A wriggling worm of a thought pushes into my head. How much has Nate told her about me and my history with The Burgess? Or even if my reputation extends beyond Nate, if my name is one whispered in corridors or the subject of drunken discussions of productions gone wrong, passed from crew to crew whenever new blood takes up residence at the playhouse. What if she is reminding me that this isn't my fault because she knows what happened before *was*?

Once again, I need to refocus myself on the task at hand. Besides, even if Eden knows of my history, she is such a seasoned pro that I doubt she would ever bring up my past like that. And if she doesn't know, the last thing I want is to introduce a new element of chaos to sow doubt into my number two.

I nibble at a lunch I grabbed from the nearby deli—a turkey sandwich with cheese. Hold the tomato, lettuce, and mayo, with mustard on the side so I can control how much is in each bite. I force myself to keep eating, even though my stomach constantly threatens to stage a revolt.

While waiting for 3:00 p.m. to roll around, I sit in my apartment, re-reading and highlighting the script. There are a few areas I want to focus on beyond the small set of pages the potential actresses have been given ahead of time. I want to be sure they can handle the full range of the Wife character, which is hard to do after hearing just one scene performed. But every time I start to focus on the story, I get distracted by sounds in and around the complex.

Maintenance is on the first floor, cleaning up Danny's apartment. Elaine is on a marathon video chat with her husband, reliving the events of last night over and over again. Alex is watching something on TV, which somehow manages to top the vacuums in Danny's room. But what distracts me the most, above all the attempts at coping and fixing last night, is a new sound I know is coming from the apartment next door.

It sounds like an electronic kids toy, one that was popular before iPads took over the brain of every child I see in restaurants and airports. A grating voice gives constant commands over a crackling snare beat, followed by a smack, a slide wheel, or a cartoon *sproing*.

I try to ignore it as long as I can. The room next to me is supposed to be empty. But the stress of the impending auditions mixed with the boldness which accompanies daylight gets me out of my chair and ready to investigate the supposedly vacant apartment next door.

I make the short ten-foot journey from my room to the next. The curtains are drawn; lights are off. But when I press my ear against the window, my suspicions are confirmed. I know this toy, remember it from a time I cannot pinpoint, an era gone by. A Bop It!. The thing never shuts up, and now I can hear it more clearly.

"Bop it, twist it, pull it, flick it, bop it, bop it, bop it."

I decide to confront whoever is inside. Someone is living next door, and it's not anyone from our cast. Whether they are squatters, performers for an upcoming show, or just friends of the owner, someone is in there.

I knock on the door.

No one answers.

I wait, knock again.

Whoever is inside is unperturbed by my calling, and the game continues unabated.

I press my face against the glass, trying to peer through a narrow gap in the curtains. With my hands cupped over my eyes to reduce glare, I am able to make out the shape of a boy sitting on the floor and a colorful toy shaped like a driver's wheel.

He is maybe ten. There is a faint light cast on him from behind, though I cannot tell if it is from the back windows of the apartment or a standing lamp nearby. But the canned overhead lights are off.

Not content to leave it there, I knock on the window. "Hello? Hey, kid, are your parents home?"

The boy shoots his gaze up from the toy, straight at me. His face is awash in surprise. Without wasting a second, he leaps to his feet and sprints across the room, outside of my narrow field of vision.

"Hello? My name is Mike O'Brien. I'm directing *Wherever You Are* at the playhouse. Is anyone else in there?"

Silence. Even the game is finally quiet.

I consider knocking on the door again, but I'm hit with a moment of clarity regarding my situation. An unknown adult staring through a window, shouting for a kid who is clearly alone to come to the door. However scared I was the other night, he is probably ten times more afraid. His parents are obviously out. If I was a kid and a stranger came creeping around my temporary lodging, I would probably bolt too.

At the very least, this confirms that I'm not going insane, that someone *is* staying next door. Just as I am making a mental note to ask about it later, my phone buzzes in my pocket. It's Eden.

"Hello?"

"Mike, where the hell are you?"

I step away from the neighbor's apartment, confused by the question. "What do you mean?"

"It's 3:15. You were supposed to be here a half hour ago. Everyone's waiting on you."

That can't be right. It has only been twenty minutes at most since I got back from the deli. Auditions aren't for another two hours.

I pull the phone away from my face, and a streak of panic peals through me. She's right. Where the hell did the time go? I planned on getting to the rehearsal space no later than 2:30 to prepare. Last I knew, it wasn't even 1:00.

"Oh my god, I'm so sorry. I'll be right there."

I hang up, dash into my room to grab my script and bag, make sure the burners are off and the fridge door is sealed, then hightail it to the rehearsal basement as fast as I can.

I am in such a hurry to rush down the four flights of stairs that I nearly forget the cadence of even-to-odd ratio and screw up the audition even further. Despite the winter weather outside, sweat is beading down my forehead when I pass through the common room.

Four women who might as well be sisters are sitting in a row of chairs with their backs against the wall. Three are studying a sheet of paper, while a fourth is staring at the vaulted ceiling. My red-faced moment is not only prolonged, but exacerbated when I make a mandatory detour past them to the break room, where I quickly tug the fridge door open and close it.

"Sorry about that," I say in the rehearsal area, nearly collapsing into my chair next to Eden and Nate. I quickly unpack my bag and align my black and red pen in a proper order—vertically next to the yellow notepad sitting slightly offset beneath my script, allowing for maximum space efficiency.

"Jesus, Mike. You doing okay?" Nate asks. The concern on his face is as plain as the sandwich I didn't eat for lunch.

"Sorry. Somehow, time got away from me. Don't ask. I couldn't tell you."

"You sure you're up for this? Eden and I can–"

"I'm good," I say, cutting Nate off. "Just a little flustered. But I'm ready. Let's send the first girl in."

Eden passes me a four-page stapled resume packet detailing each of the four contenders. It's something I should have studied before they even arrived. No time but I trust Eden when she says they are all properly vetted. My main concern has to be how appropriate they are for the role.

Eden steps out of the room for a second and calls the first actress. I'm still catching my breath from rushing over, and when I look at her face, I nearly fall out of my seat. For just a moment, I swear I'm looking at Cassandra from approximately one day ago. She is a dead ringer for the injured woman. But I can't allow looks to play too large a part in this. The main goal here is talent over beauty.

"Hi. I'm Maggie Jones. Auditioning for the role of Wife," the woman says before leading into the scene. She reads her part while Eden gives the lines for Husband. This woman not only looks like Cassandra; it's almost as if she is doing an impression of her.

In another world, this may have been a good reading, perhaps even a great one. But the woman makes it nearly impossible not to conjure an apples-to-apples comparison to her predecessor. In that regard, she is lesser on every conceivable level. I have additional scenes and questions prepared, but by the time she is finished with her two-page sample, I have seen enough.

"Thank you, Maggie, for your time and coming on such short notice. We'll let you know."

This is the part where I give a performance. From my years of experience working with actors, there are few worse feelings than knowing you have disappointed a director in your audition. It's my job to make her believe she has a chance, even when I know she is not right for the role.

In my personal opinion, it would be better to know outright if it is not happening rather than hand out false hope. But I am sitting on the other end of a table, which might as well be as far as the divide in the Grand Canyon.

We call in the next actress. Much like Maggie, this woman appears perfect for the role, at least as I have come to know it. However, she moves with confidence, striding in like a lioness headed toward her prey. She reaches her mark—an X on the ground in green gaff tape—rolls her shoulders back, and introduces herself as Kelly Argin. Something about the way she presents herself gives me immediate hope that she has her own take on the character, and I am excited to see it.

Unfortunately, as soon as the scene starts, it's as if she dons a cartoonish mask of woe. The emotion comes on too strong, too forced. The character feels disingenuous, as if there is an undercurrent of emotional manipulation to Wife instead of genuine vulnerability.

I stop her midway through and can feel Nate giving me a look of irritation in my periphery. Clearly, he was enjoying her performance. Either that or he thinks I am being rude. But I don't care. I am here for a job, and despite all my personal problems, I'm very good at what I do.

"Kelly, can we go back to the top? But pull back about twenty percent on the emotion? I like your energy, but we want to see you take a journey to get there. Start with a low simmer and let it build to that boiling point."

Kelly nods, her eyes fierce with determination. She is a professional. The question is whether she understands the note.

The answer comes quickly. She does not.

What we get is nearly an exact repeat of her first attempt. The only difference is she starts out slightly quieter this time. By her third line, she is right back to the same melodrama which pervaded her first attempt.

I have seen enough, but I let her finish the audition, then excuse her, tossing in a compliment that her second take was "much closer to what we're looking for." Kelly gives a single, strong nod, then strides back out of the room.

"I liked her," Nate says once the door is shut.

I fight back a wince. Ultimately, the decision comes down to me, but as the writer, his perspective needs to be taken into account. Instead of sharing my real feelings, I lie to him, just the same as I did to Kelly. Partially to keep him happy, and partly because, when I look into his eyes, I feel a pang of guilt from accusing him of reneging on his sobriety the other day when, in fact, I was the one drinking last night.

We bring in the third girl. I immediately recognize her as the only one who was not studying her script when I first came in.

Most actors walk in as a bundle of nerves, doing their best to hide their anxiety and present themselves as someone ready for the job. When you have worked as long as I have, you can catch every tell, from fidgety hands to fake humility, to an air of overconfidence, like the previous actress. But there is something different about this woman, a certain quiet stillness inside of her while she takes her time to cross the room and reach her designated position.

She doesn't greet us upon entry. The woman simply walks, as if she were strolling through the park without anyone watching her at all. It isn't until she is facing us that I even get a good look at her face.

Much like her movement, there is a calm beauty to her, something natural in her bright blue eyes which genuinely gives me a feeling like she doesn't have a care in the world.

Before she introduces herself, she takes a moment to look each of us in the eyes, starting with Eden and ending with me. Everything an actor does from the moment they enter a room until they leave is a tell. It informs us not just who they are as a performer, but how they approach their craft, whether they will be easy or difficult to work with, and how well they can take direction.

Something as seemingly simple as eye contact can speak volumes about an actor. Too quick a glance shows a nervous display of respect or possibly desperation. Too long can show defiance and be an early sign of high maintenance. Some people have the thousand-yard stare, where they are so nervous that they look right through you to the door they are going to cycle back to in short order.

But not her.

Instead of trying to be noticed, she makes *me* feel seen. It is a rare and refreshing quality in an actor. If she can connect this quickly with the three of us, then she can connect with a packed house of audience members and draw them into her character with nothing more than a glance.

She is older than the others, probably in her early thirties, while the rest were all mid-twenties. There is no way of dressing her down to look the same age as Alex, but since his character is having an affair with a boss nearly fifteen years older than him, it feels somewhat believable. And it is something I never considered before but seems right.

"Hello, my name is Bitsie Brenner," she says.

In my years I have heard some unique names, but "Bitsie" is a first.

Eden pipes up, noticing Bitsie doesn't have her script with her. "Do you need sides?"

Bitsie shakes her head. "No, I'm good."

"We haven't given you much time to prepare. It's perfectly fine to do a reading today," Eden says.

"Thank you, but I'm ready."

There is nothing braggadocious in her words. She doesn't sound as if she is showing off, simply stating a fact. The way she speaks has a natural sadness to it. Not in a depressing way, but perhaps just a little world-weary. It's how Wife is written, and I genuinely cannot tell if she is putting on an act or if this is really her.

"Nice to meet you, Bitsie," I say. "Let's get right to it then, shall we?"

Her audition brings the exact same energy as her introduction, and by the end of her first run-through, I am even more lost as to whether she has been performing since the moment she walked in. Her take on the role is very different from what we have been working with.

Cassandra played the role as a woman desperate to cling to her marriage and a sense of normalcy. Like she was always trapped on the precipice of a cliff, fighting back a hurricane which constantly threatened to send her life hurtling down into a pit of despair. Bitsie, on the other hand, plays the role with a more reserved intensity, as someone who is constantly compartmentalizing her traumas like she is filling up a filing cabinet, unknowing of when it will overflow. It's restrained but also more believable. She teeters the line of stability with a question of *if* she will reach her boiling point rather than *when.*

It serves as a good reminder that we aren't trying to cast a carbon copy of Cassandra. We are going all the way back to square one—finding the perfect fit for the role of Wife. There are any number of factors in delivery, emotion, and unnamable energy which might make someone the right fit for a role, and they may be very different from what Cassandra brought to the table. I need to remain open to a new interpretation of the character instead of a replication of what I'm used to.

In the end, my biggest concern is it might be a performance so nuanced that it would be better for the screen than for audience members viewing her all the way from the balcony. But then I catch her eyes again and can't help but feel like she is speaking directly to me, experiencing the emotion in real time, baring vulnerability without broadcasting it.

My other worry is that Alex is going to seem too over-the-top next to her. I am struggling to recontextualize the whole play to match Bitsie instead of fitting her like a piece into the puzzle we have already half assembled.

"I want her," I say the moment Bitsie leaves the room. "She's perfect."

"Well, she's certainly different," Nate says.

I try to read the tone of his voice. It's not a *no,* but he will need more convincing. Instead of forcing my opinions on him, I let him take the lead.

"Give me your thoughts," I say.

"I don't know. She's just not quite how I envisioned the character. She's a little too put together."

"It's definitely a new approach to the character," Eden adds.

I nod, finding Nate's criticism to be the very cornerstone of my sudden infatuation. "I agree completely, but don't you think it makes for a more interesting juxtaposition to Alex? He plays the role like a guy who's checked out, right? He's acting out, not addressing the miscarriage, having an affair with his boss...And she's the one who forces him to get his shit together when they move to the farm in Act 2. The audience expects her to be the total opposite force of him, desperate for his attention. What if we had someone who seemed stronger than him and is only brought to a boiling point when his antics force it out of her? That way, she's less of a Chekov's gun and more of a fleshed-out character with her own autonomy?"

Nate narrows his lips, and I worry I have insulted his writing and characterization with my recontextualization. But at the same time, I have also pointed out the problem with overconfident Kelly, who he previously said was his top pick. She played the role like a caricature, while Bitsie felt *real*.

"You've worked with her before. What's she like?" I ask Eden.

"She's only done one show with me before. About five years ago, she was Blanche in *Brighton Beach Memoirs*. She was a bit of a perfectionist, but aside from that, there were no complaints."

In that play, Blanche is a widow and mother living off her parents and struggling to find her own voice. Emotionally, it's not too far of a cry from the Wife in *Wherever You Go*.

Nate nods, and I believe he is coming to the same conclusion as me. "Okay, not bad. Let's wait to see how number four does."

The first smile of the day bubbles up from my chest. I tamp it down to keep from overplaying my hand. "Great. Let's move on."

I can't even remember the final girl's name two seconds after she says it. While she lacks the overconfidence of Kelly, her audition is almost identical.

Once again, I fight the urge to grin when I glance at Nate. This woman is only illustrating my point further. She is overdramatic to the point of farce whereas Bitsie brings a refinement to the role we are not getting from these other women.

It only takes a few seconds after what's-her-name leaves for Nate to confirm what I already know. "All right, Mike. You were right."

Finally, I am allowed to celebrate a ray of light in the middle of this downpour.

"There's a reason you wanted me for this. Trust me, she's going to be–" I cut myself off before I say *better than Cassandra*. Instead, I settle for—"great. She's going to be great."

Spontaneous Writing: Session 5

Could it be, you've done some right
After what seems like endless night
Pieces break, pieces fall
But is there a reason to it all?
A ray of hope amidst the night
Keeping you in the fight
For every mistake, for every failure
A brand new chance to find new flavor
Things are falling into place
Arent you glad you joined this race?
After darkness comes the dawn
Every bird must sing its song
Now comes time to make amends
More than a means to an end
Just don't forget your real task here
Is killing Beth, that much is clear
Keep your head on, fix it straight
Dont forget, you can't fight fate
You've got her right within your grasp
See how long the fun can last

Savor til her final breath
Get ready to avenge all of our deaths
Mother, father, little boy
Fell in her arms, the end of joy
But now comes chance to make it neat
Carrots and cheese, carrots and cheese

CHAPTER 5

Eden and I call Bitsie almost immediately after concluding the auditions. She is thrilled to learn she got the part and excited to jump in tomorrow.

While Eden drafts up contracts for Bitsie to sign first thing in the morning, I return to Greenwood Terrace, planning to revise our rehearsal schedule to accommodate her addition. The plan was originally to jump straight into Act 2, then spend extra time backfilling everything Bitsie missed. But based on her new approach to the character, I am brimming with ideas on improvements—some subtle, some more noticeable—to the blocking of Act 1 as well.

I have a strict color-coding system when it comes to tracking notes, blocking, changes, and ideas on the script. It has been a long time since I have been able to break out the green pen, which is reserved for late-game notes and alterations.

The timing will be tight; we are only days away from moving into the theater for tech. By that time, the performances are supposed to be airtight, prepared for lighting and sound, and ready for the crew to work on the technical aspects of the play. At this point, we are likely going to lose at least three days of run-throughs, but it is a gamble I am hoping will pay off in service of a better result.

I am so excited by this injection of energy that I have somehow managed to slough off all my other worries. If anything, I am excited for the challenge of tackling a truncated timeline. In the world of theater, there are a million problems which can crop up at any time, from minuscule to massive. Rising to the occasion of sudden collapse and chaos is built into us—one of the strange, masochistic joys of working in a live medium. It is one of the only art forms in which catastrophe becomes an opportunity to elevate.

The sun begins to set, melting away the harsh orange light pouring through my window. It is only when I get up to turn on the light switch that I hear a commotion coming from outside.

When I peer through my window, I spot Alex Keating on the sidewalk, losing his mind at the vagrant I encountered the other night. The whites in the man's eyes are visible from here, hidden behind a layer of grime. He is not backing down, and if I didn't know any better, I would say these two are about to come to blows.

I hurry down the stairs, noting Danny and Elaine standing in their doorways, watching the fight unfold. Elaine has her camera pointed at the action, surely relaying the altercation in real time on a video call with her husband.

"What the hell's going on?" I ask Danny while I pass his apartment.

"Drama. And I am here for it." His arms are crossed and his eyes fixed dead ahead. He wears a smug grin. The only thing he looks like he is missing is a bucket of popcorn.

"Not helpful." I rush forward to interject myself between the two shouting men. "Alex, what are you doing!" I grab him by the shoulders and pull him back while he jabs a finger at the other man.

"I've already called the cops," he hisses, but I am not sure if it is directed toward me or the other guy.

"Why? What happened?"

For a moment, Alex regards me, still pointing an accusatory finger in front of him. "This homeless bum is the fucker who broke into my apartment. He's literally wearing my Marc Jacobs right now."

"I think the preferred term is 'unhoused,'" Danny calls from his doorway, cupping his hands around his mouth to mimic a megaphone.

"Fuck off, Danny. I don't care about your PC bullshit right now.

The asshole's homeless, and he stole my stuff. That's *my* hoodie he's wearing!" Alex grabs the man's sweatshirt. It is a black piece of clothing covered in vertical columns of letters spelling "MARC."

The vagrant not only slaps Alex's hand away; he grips him by the wrist and twists, sending Alex spinning around and dropping to his knees to avoid any broken bones.

"I already warned you once, man. Don't touch me. You shove me again and I will end you," the vagrant says.

"Do you all hear that? He's threatening me!" Alex shouts. "He's threatening my life! I've got witnesses, pal!"

"Hey..." I keep my hands up, fingers splayed to show I am not a threat, while pushing myself between the two. Adrenaline pumps through me, and my director's conflict resolution instincts kick in, overriding any of my own concerns for personal safety. "Let's all just relax a little here, okay? My name's Mike. What's yours?"

"My name is Legion, for I am many. But you can call me Steve."

"Okay, Steve. How about you let go of my friend here and I'll make sure he doesn't touch you again? Is that all right with you?"

I wouldn't consider myself a particularly big man. There is nothing about me which would make anyone think I could win a physical fight against pretty much anyone. But I do know how to speak with calm authority. It works, and Steve releases Alex's hand, managing to also shove him a few steps away in the process.

Steve threatens Alex now that he has let him go. "He better not touch me again. I don't want nobody touching me. I served in the U.S. military for twenty years. I deserve respect."

"Okay." I nod. "No one's going to touch you, right, Alex?" I give Keating a look. If I know anything, it is how to convey a message with just an expression.

Alex is still steaming, but he steps back and rubs at his wrist. "Fine. We'll let the police sort it out when they get here."

Now that the immediate threat of violence is over, I try to take stock of the situation. The sweater Steve is wearing *does* appear expensive. It barely has a stain on it, which is a sharp juxtaposition to his ragged pants and decomposing shoes exposing his bare toes. His shopping cart is similarly spotted with a few brightly colored objects contrasted against a beige sleeping bag, a filthy backpack, and wads of dirt-encrusted clothes.

"Steve, where did you find these clothes?" I ask.

Steve shrugs and sniffs up a rumbling loogie. "Around. The sweater was just sitting in the bushes up the block. Found the rest in a dumpster out back."

"Bullshit!" Alex calls out. "Where's my laptop? Is it hiding somewhere in your basket, or did you already hock it for meth money?"

"I didn't find no laptop, and I ain't a thief."

"We'll just see about that," Alex spits.

A police cruiser pulls up, its red and blue lights highlighting the whole building on the rapidly darkening street. In the complex across from us, gawkers' faces are temporarily bathed in the swirling flashes while they stare out their windows.

Two police officers exit the vehicle. One immediately approaches Steve while the other turns to me. Either I give off an air of someone who can adequately fill them in on the story or I seem pretentious enough to have been the one who called them.

I direct the officer to Alex, who opens with, "I want to press charges."

While the cops are conducting their separate interviews, a voice echoes from up the street with a gasp. "Oh my god!"

It is the last person I expect to see—and at the worst possible time.

It is Bitsie Brenner.

To my surprise, she approaches the vagrant first. "Are you all right, Steve?"

He nods. "According to this fancy fuck, I broke into his place and stole his stuff. But I didn't do nothing."

A troubled look draws her face down, and she shakes her head. "Officer, I know this man. He has his troubles, but Steve's not the type to burglarize."

"Hey, bitch," Alex says. "Why don't you mind your own business?"

"Excuse me?" Bitsie directs her attention to Keating. "That's no way to talk to a stranger. I'm just trying to help."

"And who the hell are you? Go home, lady."

"I live around the block, and I actually take the time to get to know the people in my neighborhood. Steve saved me once by scaring off a mugger on my way home one night."

"Well, isn't that great for you," Alex says with a sneer.

I walk as quickly as possible over to Alex. "Sorry, officer. Can I borrow him for just a second?"

The officer nods. I place a hand on Alex's back and walk him up the block.

"Alex Keating, meet your new Wife, Bitsie Brenner."

Alex has been beet red since the moment I stepped outside, but it only takes five seconds for all the color to drain from his face.

"Oh, fuck me. I'm so sorry. I had no idea." He nearly trips over himself to make amends.

"Clearly," Bitsie replies.

"I'd be lying if I said this is how I hoped our two leads would meet," I say, trying to ease the tension. "Bitsie, what are you doing here?"

"Like I said, I live nearby. I thought I might stop by and see if anyone was in the common area outside. Just hoping to meet some of my new castmates."

"Listen, I'm not normally an asshole," Alex says. "It's just that my apartment got broken into recently and I've been seeing this homeless guy creeping around...And now I caught him wearing my stuff."

"You know, the preferred term is 'unhoused.'"

"I tried to tell him the same thing." Danny now stands only a few feet away.

Bitsie's face morphs from distaste to near elation. She looks over and bursts into laughter. "*Danny Sparks*?" They give each other an aggressive embrace. "What's it been? Six, seven years?"

"Too long, my darling! How are you?"

"Better now." She casts a side-eye at Alex, whose attention has been pulled back to the officer.

"You two know each other?" I ask.

"Heck yeah, we do!" Danny beams. "We were in *Taming of the Shrew* at the Seattle Rep. She's my sister from another mister."

"Well, I'm glad at least some of our cast can get off on the right foot."

"I can fill you in on *everything* that's been going on," Danny says, turning to Bitsie. "If you need any extra time to go over blocking, rehearsal notes, anything, I've got all the tea. Why don't you come on in? I'll mix us some drinks, and we can catch up. Don't mind the blood on the rug." They head toward his unit, and he calls up a floor. "Elaine, come meet Bitsie. You're going to *love* her!"

With Danny keeping Bitsie entertained, I return my attention to the police matters.

"Can you prove that these articles belong to you?" the officer is asking.

Alex chews his lip and darts his eyes around, like he is searching through a mental storage unit. His eyebrows jump in a moment of realization. "Yes! I think I got my receipt emailed to me." He pulls out his phone and starts furiously scrolling through his inbox. "Here." Alex shows the officer. "A Marc Jacobs cotton sweatshirt. That's $398 plus tax."

The cop nods. "And you say he broke in through your window?"

"Cut open the mesh while I was at rehearsal. This is just one of over a dozen things that were taken. All *very* expensive."

The officer goes to confer with his cohort, who is wearing rubber gloves and rifling through the contents of the shopping cart. "Sir, can you join us over here?" he says to Alex.

There is a heap of expensive-looking clothes next to a collection of ratty objects that have seen better years.

"Is this everything that was stolen from your dwelling?" the officer asks.

"No. I had a MacBook and some other stuff. I'm still trying to account for everything."

The officer turns to Steve. "And do you have any way to prove that you found these items where you say you did?"

"Oh!" Steve snaps his fingers. "I *did* find a stupid-looking green fuzzy bucket hat in the dumpster that I didn't take. Might still be there."

Alex's jaw drops open. "That's a Loro Piana you're talking about! And it's *not* stupid; it's *fashionable*. I wore that to the Golden Globes two years ago."

One officer goes around the back of the building to check the dumpster and quickly returns with said hat. "Is this it?"

Steve is right. It *does* look stupid.

Alex nods grudgingly. "Yes."

"Okay, then," the officer says. "So, we checked through this man's things and were unable to find a knife or implement that could cut through a window screen. We also didn't find any laptops. Paired with the hat he describes from the dumpster, we're unable to prove theft at this time."

"You have to be kidding. So you're just going to do *nothing*?" Alex moans.

"Well, you were able to reasonably prove that you purchased these items, so if you want them back, we can have them confiscated from Steve here and returned to you."

Alex recoils in disgust. "Ew! I don't want to touch any of that. It's all been mixed in with his filth."

"In that case, there's not much more we can do at this time. We recommend you keep your doors and windows locked and try to keep all valuables hidden from sight, so as not to attract any more potential burglars."

Alex sighs, shaking his head. "But he threatened me! Everyone heard it. He said he was going to kill me."

"From our notes, it sounds like that only happened *after* you physically assaulted him. That technically makes you the aggressor. Thankfully for you, Steve here has decided not to press charges at this time."

The fire flares back up Alex's cheeks. "*Thankfully for me*? You've got to be kidding. This would *never* happen in Los Angeles. Thanks for nothing." He storms back into his apartment and slams the door behind him.

"Thank you, officers. Sorry about all this," I say.

After another minute, they return to their car and drive off.

"Hey, guy... Thanks for stepping in there." Steve loads his stuff from the sidewalk back into his cart.

"I'm Mike. I'm sorry things got as heated as they did," I say.

"You know, if he kept pushing, I would have done it. I'm not lying about being in the service." Steve digs through his backpack, unzips a side pocket, and produces a small switchblade the police must have missed during their search. It has dirt-encrusted filigree etched on both ends of the handle and a faded picture of an eagle with the American flag in its mouth.

My pulse quickens when he casually flicks out the blade and shows it to me.

Steve tucks it back into his bag. "You're one of the good ones. I can tell these things. If you're ever in trouble, I got your back."

"Uh, thanks," I say, now all kinds of conflicted.

Steve begins to push his cart up the hill, muttering one last thing before heading down the alley. "Oh...and don't forget to kill Beth."

For approximately two hours, things were coming together. I was able to forget my personal problems and focus on *Wherever You Go*. But now, while I count the stairs on the way back up to my unit, I catch a quick glimpse of a man pulling the door to the neighboring apartment closed.

I consider knocking and introducing myself, but instead, a whole new host of worries swirls in my head. The ending of my encounter with Steve has me shaken. Something about the way he so calmly displayed the knife was even more frightening than if he had done it with any sort of aggression. He spoke with such ease about killing Alex if provoked, the same way I would tell someone I might grab a coffee later if I was feeling tired.

I believe he would. And for a second time now, I am sure he said, "Kill Beth."

What if he really was the person who broke into Alex's unit? And for that matter, what if he broke into mine? Despite Bitsie's claims of his harmlessness, Steve is clearly capable of much more. But I don't know his agenda. What if he has been in here, rummaging through my stuff, reading my spontaneous writing sessions just to mess with me?

I try to summon the non-conspiracy-prone part of my mind to figure out why anyone would do something like that. What possible reason could Steve have to read through my ramblings? But it is hard to reject insane-sounding propositions when I am checking my stovetop knobs for the fifth time today to make sure I didn't leave the gas on, especially when I have not used the appliance a single time since I have been here.

It also doesn't help that any effort to pivot my focus back onto work brings up an entirely new concern.

The saying "First impressions are everything" exists for a reason. In my job, first impressions are generally all I have to go on when casting. I must make a million small decisions a day, and if I don't trust my gut—my first impressions—I would never get anything done.

The initial interaction between Bitsie and Alex could not have gone worse. I was planning on bringing pastries to tomorrow's rehearsal and spending the first half hour of the morning giving the actors time to get to know Bitsie and vice versa. In my head, I had built a controlled environment where, as the director, I could steer things the right way.

It is hard enough replacing an actor midway through the process and even worse in the wake of such a traumatic incident. Cliques form, even in a small cast. I wanted to bring everyone together for a fresh start and be as ready as possible to create chemistry between them before having the cast step into character.

This new meet and greet is even more important, given the amount of green ink I have already dedicated to re-shaping so much of the script. The last thing I want is for the actors to resent Bitsie for being a catalyst of so many changes throughout the show. And, of course, the person most affected by these alterations is Alex, who shares nearly every scene in the play with her.

The fact they got off on an antagonistic foot has me deeply concerned about their first personal meeting pouring into their professional relationship.

Even now, laughter resonates in the unit directly below me, where Bitsie and Danny are reminiscing about their good old days. This means Alex can hear them too, from his room where he is most certainly stewing in his own anger.

I consider heading down to talk to him directly, but meetings like this are the exact reason why directors are normally lodged off-site from their cast. Alex is not my friend; I am his boss. We are not at rehearsal. Therefore, it would be inappropriate for me to just drop by.

I need help and advice on what to do, how to handle this situation. But much like it would be unprofessional for me to reach out to Alex, it would be improper for me to contact Dr. Jules outside of our scheduled appointments.

That leaves Nate.

I shoot him a text.

> You had dinner yet?

Almost immediately, three dots appear on my phone, indicating he is composing a response to my message.

> Was just scrounging around my pantry.
> What's up?

> You want to grab a bite and go over the new plan for the show? My treat.

> Yeah. Where you want to go?

> Anywhere but Shakespeare's Head.

Fifteen minutes later, I am standing outside Nacho Mama's Cafe. It is a Mexican restaurant, mostly a tourist spot, but it is also a simple seven-minute walk from both Greenwood Terrace and Nate's apartment. Any time I am on the West Coast, I try to eat Mexican food as much as possible. It is not quite the hub, like LA or San Diego, but the food is better than anything I would find in Atlanta or New York.

I am the first to arrive. The tables for two are a bit cramped. I have my trusty bag with me and want plenty of space to go over my script without worrying about spilling food on it, so I request a table for four. By the time I have unpacked my pens, aligned them properly, and made it through another three pages of the script, Nate plops down in a chair across from me.

"We having a party?"

It takes me a second to get what he means. "Oh, no. Just wanted to have room to work."

Nate produces an almost invisible sigh. "Of course. Always work. Please don't take this the wrong way, but do you do anything *other* than work these days?"

People often use the phrase "I feel seen" in a positive manner, and I envy them.

I try to answer in the least pathetic way possible so we can move forward with the conversation. "I read books. Sometimes, I like to paint, but I'm not very good at it."

"But like, socially...You don't ever just hang out for the sake of hanging out? Just with friends?"

Once again, honesty is the best policy, even if it is depressing. "You and my therapist are probably the closest friends I have."

"Jesus, that's kind of grim. I'm a terrible friend." Nate grins, probably trying to lighten the mood. "What's on your mind?"

"I want to talk about Bitsie. You've trusted me so far when it comes to what's best for the show. I've spent the evening going through the script, and I think we need to do some serious re-work of the blocking in Act 1 and approach some of the material in Act 2 differently, based on Bitsie's performance." I pass him my papers. "Everything marked in green is where I think we need to change things up."

Nate spends a minute turning through a few pages, squinting to read my chicken scratch handwriting. "Shit. I wasn't sure during the audition, but I think you're right. This is better. So, what's the problem?"

"Well, as you've just helped me illustrate, I'm not the best when it comes to relationships with people. And we sort of had an incident right before I texted you that I think might make implementing these changes a problem."

I tell Nate the story of Alex, Steve, and Bitsie, sparing no detail except for the parts with the knife and Steve's suggestion to kill my imaginary enemy, Beth. Despite Nate's extroverted personality and his ability to blend into any room or conversation with ease, he is an anxious person. Maybe even as apprehensive as me. He can see where I am headed miles before I get there.

When I reach the end of my story, I ask, "Do you think this is going to be a problem, or am I crazy?"

"Nah. It's definitely going to be a problem. Alex is high-maintenance to begin with. He's not going to like us curtailing his performance to cater toward a vibe that better suits the newcomer. Even if it *is* the right move."

"So, what do we do?"

Nate sucks his teeth, making a loud snapping sound. He flips back through the pages of the script. "Well, you can't tell Alex any of this."

"Thanks for your insight," I say with a smirk.

"For reals, though. It took me a minute to come around to Bitsie, I think the best course is to keep doing what you're doing and hope Alex gets onboard. If he doesn't, then we have a new conversation."

Nate has successfully confirmed what my gut has been telling me. For the moment, I feel marginally better about that situation. But I hesitate to bring up the other thing on my mind. I owe it to him, especially after my unintentional alcohol slip-up.

"Listen, I wanted to apologize for how I acted last week. For accusing you of organizing the actors to ambush us at dinner...and particularly for questioning your sobriety. I was an asshole, and I let intrusive thoughts win."

Nate swats at the air. "Come on, man. It's already forgotten. We're good."

"Seriously, it was really inappropriate, and I just wanted to say I'm sorry."

"Eh, you know me," Nate says. "It's water under the bridge."

His words bring me more relief than I expected. I hadn't realized how much I was holding onto bad emotions regarding that exchange until the moment Nate gave me permission to let them go. But though I want to go a step further and tell him about my incident with alcohol, something inside of me just can't do it.

Our waitress reaches our table to take drink orders. Nate asks for a club soda with lime, and for the first time in as long as I can remember, I want nothing more than to order a pint of beer.

Spontaneous Writing: Session 6

Tacos and beer, tacos and beer
forget your worries, numb your fear
You've only got so much to lose
Why not kick back with some booze
Once you've got that perfect buzz
Smash Beths bones until they're dust
You've opened up the door so far
Run her over with a car
Then back it over once or twice
Squish her melon, won't that be nice?
Do it for Caleb, do it for me
Do it before the clock strikes three
We couldn't do it, now we're drowning in tears
Tacos and beer, tacos and beer
Couldn't stop it, no more bop it
Twist it pull it spin it drop it
Even Steve has let you know
You need to cut loose, enjoy the show
You know just what you need to do

Fuck the actors, fuck the crew
You only have to do what's best
Kill Beth
Kill Beth.

CHAPTER 6

The motion-activated floodlights outside my apartment rouse me from sleep. I rub my eyes and sit up, then clap my hands over my mouth before I can wake the entire building with a scream.

The silhouette of a man stands beyond the curtains, dead center in front of my apartment.

He is completely still, a shadow projected onto the off-white linen, which only filters so much light. My teeth chatter to no specific tune. In my head, it sounds like a horse galloping.

Five, four, one, five, four one, five, four, one, five, four, one.

My heart pounds in my chest. My legs are numb with fear. I fight to send a command from my brain.

Get up.

And do what? Hide? Attack? I don't know.

Visions of Steve waving around his knife pop into my head. Him talking with total nonchalance about how easy it would be to commit murder. Him wandering around my room, digging my spontaneous writing notes from my trash, and reading them while grinning with his blackened teeth.

Perhaps it is best if I don't move. Don't get up. He doesn't know I am awake. Maybe this is a misguided attempt to look out for me, as he said he would.

Time crawls by. I don't even think I have blinked once since noticing the silhouette. All I can do is stare at the figure stone-still on the other side of the window.

Though I am prepared to spend the rest of the night watching, the floodlight eventually clicks off. All is dark again. Somehow, this is worse. If he moves, the light will click back on.

It doesn't.

He is out there, so motionless that even infrared detectors have forgotten about him.

But not me.

Another few minutes go by.

I am fully awake, trying to come up with some sort of plan but producing nothing, unable to move, barely even breathing.

A loud thump comes from the room next to me. From one thin wall away echoes the shrill cry of a woman. She is begging, pleading. A child begins to shriek but is quickly silenced by another heavy thud.

The man outside.

Steve.

He must have broken in next door. He is hurting the people there, maybe killing them.

Before I realize it, I am on shaky legs, rushing toward my door. When I am halfway across the room, the floodlight turns back on, and I freeze in place.

The man, the shape. He is still there, standing like a statue.

It doesn't matter how scared I am. I need to find out what the hell is going on. But first, I backtrack to my kitchenette, thumb the burners, and press my hand against the fridge door. The ritual wraps me in a security blanket of false confidence. I make another approach, flipping the lock and throwing open the door, finding—

Not Steve. Not even anyone I recognize.

A man wearing glasses is leaning over the rail, in a brown checkered coat, smoking a cigarette. He turns to me, startled.

"Heavens, you scared me!" He clutches a hand to his chest.

"I'm so sorry," I say, monumentally stupid. "I saw you through the curtains. The floodlights..."

"Oh my...You must have thought I was a burglar! I'm terribly sorry." The man speaks with a British accent. There is something vaguely familiar about his face, though I can't quite place it.

"I'm Mike. Mike O'Brien." I extend a hand.

"Chester," the man says, giving me a solid shake.

His hand is nearly freezing. How cold it is out here. A shiver passes through my body, and I realize I am only dressed in a T-shirt and gym shorts in the middle of winter.

"Is everything okay in there?" I point next-door, to apartment 3B. "It sounded like screaming."

"Playing, actually. Again, I'm dreadfully sorry. We're just in from London, and the jetlag has us up at all hours. Right now, for us, it's..." He shakes his arm, and a wristwatch slides down from his coat sleeve. "It's quarter past three here, so that must be eleven in the morning for us. Nothing worse than a combination of restlessness and boredom."

I let out another sigh of relief while tension drains out of me. Even without a cigarette, a smoke-like plume of frost billows from my mouth.

"You're a director, right?" Chester asks.

"That's right." I nod. "We open in just a couple weeks. We're doing a new play called *Wherever You Go.*"

Chester shakes his head. "And here we are, keeping you up at all hours of the night."

"It's fine. Maybe just tell the wife and kid to keep it to a dull roar?"

"I'll do just that." Chester stubs his cigarette out against the railing, then drops it to the floor.

"Are you here for the next show?" I ask before he has a chance to head back into his apartment.

"Yes, but we're rather early. I'm old friends with Rebecca Burgess. We don't make it this way too often, so we thought we'd spend a few weeks catching the sights, doing a spot of traveling in the area."

So, he *is* one of Rebecca's friends. Of course, she would offer lodging to a friend if there was room.

"Anywho...I'll make sure my family keeps quiet. You won't hear another peep from us tonight. I'm sure you have another big day tomorrow."

"Always. It was great meeting you, Chester. I'm sure I'll see you around."

It isn't until I am back in my unit that I realize just how freezing I am. After tapping the stove and fridge, I nearly run across the room to bundle myself back into bed.

***

Despite the interruption in the middle of the night, I wake up early to buy coffee and a box of pastries for everyone in the rehearsal basement. Nate and Eden are already there, each scribbling on their respective notebooks.

I catch Eden up to speed on the incident between Alex and Bitsie from yesterday afternoon and, more importantly, the meeting I had with Nate regarding changes to the script. While I am sure she is bubbling with frustration over my decision to pivot the tone of the play, she doesn't let an ounce of it show. She confirms that our first half of the day will be dedicated to doing a table read, which is necessary for Bitsie but will be largely unhelpful to our other three cast members.

When Bitsie enters ten minutes early to sign paperwork, she surprises us all by already having a script in hand. "Danny took me to FedEx and made me a copy last night so I could prepare," she explains. "I've studied my lines so I can hit the ground running."

"Regardless, you should probably have a copy that isn't marked up with Danny's blocking." Eden trades Bitsie for a new one.

While I admire Bitsie's proactiveness, I can almost detect a hint of irritation finally breaking through Eden.

A few minutes later, the rest of the cast enter, and any trepidation they have about their new castmate is quickly covered by the delight of donuts and free coffee. They gorge themselves on sugar and caffeine.

Bitsie stands up and waves to everyone. "Hey! I know I met you all yesterday, but I just wanted to officially introduce myself. I'm Elizabeth Brenner. Bitsie for short."

Elizabeth.

Beth.

I choke on a sip of coffee, triggering a coughing fit which redirects all eyes toward me.

"You all right there, Mike?" Nate asks.

"Elizabeth?" I croak between coughs. "I, uh...I didn't know your name was Elizabeth."

Everyone stares at me as if I just ripped all my clothes off and pranced naked around the basement.

"Oh, yeah. But nobody calls me that. Bitsie's fine."

While she goes on to list some fun facts about herself and other plays she has been in, I lean over to Nate and Eden and whisper, "I didn't know *Bitsie* was short for *Elizabeth*."

They both shrug.

"Is there a problem?" Eden asks, detecting my obvious fear and shock.

"No." I try to recover, but it feels like someone has wrapped circles of barbed wire around my brain, throat, and lungs, then pulled them tight. "I just didn't know."

Thankfully, Eden is as sharp as ever at picking up on my body language. She basically takes over the rehearsal, announcing that we are starting with a table read and, while we do plan on blocking Act 2, we are going to spend some extra time reconfiguring a few scenes in Act 1 as well.

Meanwhile, I'm doing everything I can to focus on my breathing and fighting off a massive panic attack. I feel sick and dizzy, like I might pass out or throw up—or both at the same time.

Eden instructs everyone to open their scripts to page one and begins reading the direction. "Act 1, Scene 1. WIFE sits in a doctor's office while HUSBAND paces nervously. WIFE rubs a hand on her stomach."

"This is taking forever," Alex says impatiently, running a hand through his hair to help him get into character.

"Would you relax? Stressing more isn't going to help the doctor come in any sooner," Bitsie sounds more pleading than harping.

"How's your stomach? Are you killing Beth?"

Bile burns my throat. I scoot my chair back, afraid I might need to run to the bathroom.

"You sure you're okay?" Nate asks.

I nod and wipe beads of sweat from my forehead. "Can we take that last line again?"

"How's your stomach? Are you feeling better?" Alex repeats, this time without any substitutions pulled from my crumbling sanity.

They continue with the scene, but I am still trapped within the depths of what I just heard. The room is all at once too hot and unbearably stuffy. I shuffle out of my coat. My armpit sweat is soaking through my shirt, and drops run down my face, like condensation on a soda bottle.

I cough, unsure if it is going to be accompanied by a gallon of coffee and donuts, then lean over and whisper to Eden, "I need to step out for a minute and get some water."

"You okay?" she asks.

"Just a tickle in my throat." I slide from my chair and sneak out of the room as quickly and quietly as I can. The bathroom isn't far, and I thank the porcelain gods that I make it in time before heaving up my breakfast.

Even after violently emptying my stomach of all its contents, I'm still dying of heat. When I try to stand, the room spins, and I fall back onto my knees.

This time, I slowly stagger to my feet, running five or six repetitions of "Seven Nation Army" with my teeth. I carry myself on wobbly legs to the sink and splash water on my face.

The door behind me opens, and to my surprise, Chester walks in.

"Mikey boy, fancy meeting you here." He steps up to the counter next to me, dressed in that same brown checkered suit, which is almost a caricature of classic British design.

"Chester, what are you doing here?" I ask.

"Sorry! Didn't mean to interrupt. The wife and child are finally asleep. I figured I'd do some exploring, take a look at the rehearsal space to get a feel for it. I'm sure you know how it is—that time of solitude before everything gets too hectic to be able to stop and appreciate the moment."

"Uh huh." I barely listen. My stomach lets out a gurgle so loud I swear it echoes through the tiled room.

Between splashes of water on my face, Chester's reflection in the mirror shifts from excitement to concern. "Pardon my rudeness, but you're not looking so good. Everything all right?"

"I think I must have eaten something that's disagreeing with me." I gargle some tap water and spit it out into the basin. A long string of saliva accompanies it, like a barf bungee jumper. I have to rub my forearm against my mouth to sever the line.

"You know what always helps me? A bit of ginger ale. Wonderful for the stomach. I think I remember passing a petrol station just a block or two from here. Would you like me to fetch some for you?"

"Thanks, but I could use the fresh air," I say and mean it. I need to get out of this building, if only for a few minutes. While I don't usually fall victim to claustrophobia, being four flights of stairs underground has me feeling like I am trapped in a windowless prison.

"Hope you feel better soon!" he chimes when I exit the bathroom.

Another wave of dizziness hits me as I am circling up the spiraling staircase toward freedom. I count every step of the way to keep my head from repeating the last five minutes.

Beth. Her name is Beth, a voice keeps poking into my brain, like a needle being shoved through my eardrum. The harder I try to focus on counting stairs, the more it drones into me. *Beth, Beth, Beth, Beth.*

I clutch at the railing to keep myself from toppling, but I can't risk looking down in case I am consumed by vertigo.

Finally, I explode out the doors into the small garden behind the museum. I deeply inhale the crisp Seattle air, and my lungs burn from the rapid change in climate. My face is still drying from the sink, and water soaks into my collar, along with large pools of sweat encircling my armpits. The overwhelming heat I experienced moments ago quickly reverses into a shivering cold, with the wetness rapidly cooling against my skin.

I wish I had brought my winter coat up with me.

The mini-mart Chester was referring to isn't far, and I hurry at a brisk walk without breaking into a full-on jog.

I pull open the door with almost as much fervor as when I left the stairwell, then quickly scan the contents along the refrigerated walls. There aren't any cans, but there is an old-school green glass bottle of ginger ale over by the far corner. I grab it, along with a pack of mints to cover my puke breath and some salted crackers to help coat my stomach. After paying, I head outside and twist open the soda.

At first, I take a baby sip and wait for it to fizz its way down my esophagus and into my stomach. I count to ten with my eyes closed, waiting to see if it will cause a revolt and come right back up.

My stomach lets out a satisfied gurgle, and the pressure inside of me releases in the form of a burp. It's working. I rip open the crackers and nibble on them while I take bigger swigs of the ginger ale. By the time I return to the outside of the rehearsal center, I have nearly drunk the whole bottle. But before I reach the door, someone dressed as museum security steps in front of me.

"Hey, buddy. What do you think you're doing?"

Trying to keep these crackers down, I want to say. Instead, I shrug at him, having no idea what he is talking about.

"What's the problem?" I ask.

"What do you think?" He points at the soda in my hand.

"Oh, I'm not taking this into the museum. I'm working down in the rehearsal hall," I explain.

"It doesn't matter where you're going. You can't be drinking that in public."

Now I'm totally confused. What the hell is wrong with ginger ale?

I glance down at the green bottle, and my stomach does a backflip. Icy sweat leaks from my pores when I read the word "Heineken."

This isn't drinking ginger ale at all. It's beer. A prickling sensation runs down my neck and back, like a giant spider skittering across my flesh.

"I'm so sorry," I say. "I didn't—"

"Just toss it and move on." The guard points to a nearby trash can.

"Of course." I do as he says.

"You're lucky the police didn't see you. We take open container laws seriously around here."

"Absolutely. Sorry again." I hurry past the guard and punch in the code to the door. A red light turns as green as the beer bottle, and I head back inside.

My heart is beating a mile a minute. How could I have made such a huge mistake? It didn't even taste like beer. I tongue my mouth. The sweetness has evaporated, replaced by a sour bitterness that is unmistakably booze. Another shiver racks through my body, and this time, it is not from cold, but fear.

Am I really in such a bad headspace that I could trick my own taste buds?

It is a small miracle that I bought that pack of mints at the minimart. Personal guilt and shame aside, if Nate smelled alcohol on my breath, it would undo all the trust we have rebuilt. If Eden catches me drinking on the job, it could even get me fired. I sit down on the first stair and catch my breath, popping a mint into my mouth.

Tomorrow morning is my scheduled appointment with Dr. Jules, but I don't know if I can make it that long. She says to only call her number in an emergency.

I think this counts.

Her phone rings once, twice. Even the tone reverberates in my ear, buzzing the word *Beeeeeeth. Beeeeeeeth. Beeeeeeeth.*

Voicemail.

While Dr. Jules recites her message, I try to take a few more steadying breaths, though it might be better if I allow myself to sound as stressed as I feel. Maybe it will get her to call me back faster.

"Hi, Dr. Jules. This is Mike O'Brien. I know we're scheduled tomorrow, but something has come up, and I don't know what to do. If you could just call me back, I'd really, really appreciate it."

Leaving the message helps to calm me down a bit. It is a little like when I was first diagnosed with obsessive-compulsive disorder. Before any sort of treatment began, it was reassuring to know something *was* wrong with me and that I was going to get help for it.

All I have to do is hold on until Dr. Jules calls me back, and everything will be fine.

It has to be.

I manage to sit through the rest of the read-through without any more panic attacks. As much as I hate to admit it, I am a little looser after a few minutes—the same way I was on Monday at Danny's birthday party. The alcohol is doing what it is supposed to: relaxing my nervous system, letting me hop off the runaway carousel of cyclical ruminations for a little bit, and giving me enough distance from myself that I can focus on my job.

We break a little early for lunch. Danny and Bitsie are quick to sit with each other, excited to talk details of the play and do more catching up. Elaine and Alex rest in near silence, with Elaine talking on her phone and Alex playing games on his. It is only the first day of the new cast, but there is already a bad dynamic forming.

I was hoping Alex had apologized to Bitsie so they could have a better working relationship, but it seems that hasn't happened. Not to say it won't, but Bitsie and Danny acting like two peas in a pod is most likely going to further drive her and Alex apart. And with Elaine focusing almost all her personal time on her family back home, it only serves to isolate Alex.

Obviously, this is not an ideal situation for two lead actors who are not only playing a married couple, but partners who need to be able to trust each other to give and take when needed. If they can't find a way to make it feel believable, the audience never will.

Of course, there are notable exceptions. I can name a list as long as my arm of co-stars who couldn't stand each other but were still able to give tremendous performances. It just makes for a miserable experience for everyone in the production and oftentimes requires a referee to make judgment calls, instead of allowing the actors to explore the ins and outs of their parts.

Alex and Cassandra would go to each other's apartments after rehearsal to review, rework, and communicate the intention of each scene, not just the lines. I don't foresee any of that happening between these two. Not without a nudge in the right direction.

This is a problem, not just for the aforementioned reasons, but because Bitsie still needs to learn all of Act 1. We really don't have time to retread a full week and a half's work during scheduled rehearsal hours. In order to be ready for tech on time, I need to have them willingly going the extra mile to catch up.

While there may come a time for me to step in and have a talk with one or both of them, I decide to wait and see how they work together on the stage. Preemptively forcing resolution can sometimes be more harmful than waiting to see if things naturally get to the point of irreparable resentment.

Before we get back to work and begin blocking Act 2, I check my phone for the hundredth time in the last hour. Still no calls from Dr. Jules.

It's okay, I tell myself now that I have had some time to calm down. *I can wait until after rehearsal.*

All the concerns I had about Alex and Bitsie raise their ugly heads as soon as we start blocking. While the first act of the play has plenty of scenes with Elaine and Danny popping in, playing various characters, Act 2 mostly takes place in the rural town the couple move to. Aside from short scenes with neighbors and some phone calls to the Wife's brother, almost the entirety of the second half of the play is just the Husband and Wife dealing with the extreme highs and lows of their relationship.

Alex seems impatient, almost agitated, when I cut them off every couple of lines to instruct the two where to move, how to express each line, and what angles of emotion to bring to the scene. Normally, I wouldn't concentrate too deeply on the actual performance during blocking, reserving most of that until the actors are off-book and ready to focus purely on refining the piece. However, this play is very small in terms of choreography, which makes the seemingly mundane moments all the more important and requires the cast to physically react based on the context of what they are discussing in the scene. Add in the lost rehearsal time, and we are having to juggle multiple jobs at once.

Cassandra played Wife as a more combative person, with a fuse as short as a light switch. Bitsie, on the other hand, simmers like a kettle, slowly building pressure. It appears to give Alex a bit of tonal whiplash. He is prone to loud, occasionally over-the-top reactions, which was par for the course before. Now, his performance almost makes it seem like he is in an entirely different play from Bitsie.

He keeps glancing my way, his eyes asking me to step in and adjust her performance to match the pre-established tone. When that fails, he glances to Nate, who also remains stoic.

"I'm sorry. I have to stop," he finally says during a scene in which a wonderful day has been spoiled due to an insensitive backhanded comment Husband makes.

His character is ready to pop off, semi-subconsciously prodding at his wife until she reaches a breaking point so they can have a fight. But it's not happening. Though the words on the page have the Wife defending herself, Bitsie plays the scene as hurt instead of vindictive. It is one of the key moments Nate and I went over last night—a primary example of how the tone of the show needs to change.

"Is this how she's going to act the whole time?" Alex asks.

I was hoping we would be able to make it through blocking or at least a couple more days before being forced to address the shift in tone.

"I understand this is a little jarring," I say, warming up for my explanation. "Especially since you're coming from a place where you're used to a certain pattern of each other's reactions from Act 1, while Bitsie is coming in with her own perspective. This whole project has become a little unconventional, and believe me, we're all trying to figure our way as best we can through this adjustment period. For now, let's do our best to try and forget the baggage we carried from Act 1 and, much like your characters in this first half of Act 2, focus on building a new relationship from the ashes."

"What do you mean, forget Act 1?" Alex demands. "Are we going to be re-blocking this whole thing to revolve around her?"

"Not the whole thing. But we *are* going to go back and make some adjustments...once the two of you are able to find a rhythm that works for both of you."

I am trying my best to use diplomatic language, not just because he is right, but because I can empathize with his frustration. Up until this point, Alex *has* been doing everything right, based on the chemistry he had with Cassandra. Actors have delicate egos to begin with, and I can only imagine how unfair it feels for him to potentially have all his work scrubbed away through no fault of his own.

"This is bullshit," he says, smacking his marked-up script with his hand. "I don't know how I'm supposed to be working through the second half of a story when you're just throwing away everything that came before."

"If I'm doing this wrong, you can just let me know," Bitsie says. "I'm not familiar with how things were. Maybe I could change my delivery?"

"No—" I have to cut myself off from saying, "You're doing great," even though she is. "Let's just focus on the blocking for now, and then we can focus on re-examining specific beats later."

"But the blocking and beats go hand in hand!" Alex shouts. His voice echoes through the high-ceilinged room, making him sound larger and more volatile than he is. "If we're just going to say, 'Fuck it,' why don't I tear this script up and we start the whole thing over?"

For a minute, I almost want to concede to his demand. Part of me thinks it might be easier if we did go back to the beginning, just to appease Alex and possibly give him and Bitsie the illusion of a fresh start. Maybe it could be a rare second chance at a first impression. But then I remember our extremely tight timeframe, the conversation I had with Nate about this very thing, and my directorial gut, which has almost never let me down in nearly two decades of putting on shows.

I shake my head. "I wish we had the time, but we don't. If you want to meet up with me and Bitsie after-hours, I'm ready to make myself available. Otherwise, let's just finish blocking the rest of the play, and then we'll spend a day or two dedicated to making some appropriate tweaks to the first act. What do you say?"

Alex freezes. He narrows his eyes at me, waiting for me to back down.

I don't.

"Would I get paid for the overtime?" he asks.

Eden jumps in. "Union rules are pretty clear. This would be strictly an off-hours endeavor."

Alex seems like he is about to spit. "Fuck it. Fine. Let's just keep going, then."

The rest of rehearsal drags on. While my minor buzz wears off, my fears start to crawl back in. Twice, I nearly call Bitsie "Beth" by accident, and both times, I am completely derailed from my train of thought. I look like a complete fool until I consult my script and get back on track.

By the end of the day, my nerves are frayed, and I am exhausted. Bitsie and Danny loudly make plans for dinner between the two of them while they pack up, which, of course, spurs another scornful glance from Alex. Thank God Elaine steps in, seeing the obvious discord and taking pity on him. She invites Alex to grab drinks at Shakespeare's Head, which he accepts.

It isn't until I step outside the rehearsal hall that my phone buzzes. Four missed calls and two messages from Dr. Jules.

Dammit. I should have realized I had no reception down in that basement.

The first message offers to have a quick call with me in between patients. The second, from just twenty minutes ago, informs me she is out of the office for the rest of the day, and unless I am in a life-threatening situation, she won't be available for the rest of the night.

I chew my lip. My foot taps rapidly against the pavement.

I could really use a drink.

SPONTANEOUS WRITING: SESSION 7

Mikey boy, what have you done,
You went and spoiled all the fun
No you haven't, you did it right
You've got Beth right in your sights
Move the pieces, kill the queen
Fuck the show, steal the scene
Do it for Caleb, do it for me
It all happens for a reason, see?
Eat some dinner, have a drink
Give yourself some time to think
Carrots and cheese, potatoes and mash
Slice her face up, slit her gash
Dont listen to Nate, don't listen to doc,
Times running out, look at the clock
Gin Martini, make it neat
Pound Beths flesh into ground meat
Red Merlot, extra dry
So little time to make her die
Or maybe a chablis, with some cheese,
Cheddar gouda, maybe Brie

Brie
Oh shit
Brie
Shit shit shit shit shit
carrots and cheese carrots and cheese
carrots and Brie carrots and Brie

CHAPTER 7

"All right, Mike. You officially have me concerned," Dr. Jules says. It is Friday morning, and I have just finished catching her up on everything that has happened since our last appointment.

The accident with Cassandra.

Casting Bitsie, who turned out to be Beth.

My drinking...

And finally, we talked about what happened to Brie—the whole reason I left Seattle in the first place all those years ago.

"Let's take these one by one, okay? There's a lot to unpack here," Dr. Jules says.

"Okay, yeah." My leg bounces like a jackhammer. "Let's start with the part in my writing session about the broken glass, immediately preceding Cassandra's accident. That's the second time I wrote about something that then happened. First, I wrote about cutting the window's mesh. Now this. What if...I don't know...I'm subconsciously sabotaging things? What if I broke into Alex's apartment and I just don't remember? What if I slid the glass door closed on the fireplace?"

Dr. Jules has moved from emails to actual printouts of my spontaneous writing sessions. She flips through pages while I talk. Meanwhile,

I have shredded the only page I ever printed and have started taking my laptop with me wherever I go.

"I understand that you're worried you're somehow manifesting these things, but you need to step back and look at this logically. Why would you have broken into Alex's room?"

"I don't know!" My eyes are bugging out in my camera's reflection of our video chat. It doesn't help me appear like I am making a rational argument. "I don't know why I would be doing *any* of it!"

"We've already talked about this, but I think it's time for a reminder. You have a mental disorder, Mike. One that makes you predisposed to seek out patterns or find meaning in things that have no real-world significance. Alex's apartment was broken into while you were at rehearsal, right?"

My head is so frazzled I can't even remember. "I think so. But I was late to work that day. Maybe I could have done it after everyone had left."

"Do you recall going into his apartment at any time?" she asks.

"No."

"And the fireplace...Did you shove Cassandra's head into the glass?"

"No, but I started the fire..."

"Did you even recommend that she go near it?"

"No, but it was bound to happen at some point—"

She stops me by putting up a hand. "*What* was bound to happen?"

"The glass would break."

"Okay. First of all, even if you *had* slid the glass door over the fireplace, which you said you have no recollection of doing, it was not bound to shatter, especially in the way you describe. Most glass over fireplaces is tempered so that it doesn't break like that. This was a freak accident. Furthermore, you in no way coerced or even suggested that anyone stand in front of it at any time. Sometimes, bad luck is just bad luck."

I want to fight her on this, though there is no way I can articulate this deep, innate feeling that I am somehow responsible.

"Let's move on to the alcohol. This is where I'm starting to get concerned. I can see how the first incident wouldn't be your fault. I've walked by those seltzer drinks at the store and almost bought one myself once, thinking it was non-alcoholic. What bothers me is the mini-mart incident. Are you positive you weren't drinking a beer, or did you just want to *believe* you weren't drinking?"

"Hand to God, I had no idea it was beer until the guard stopped me. I swear it even tasted like ginger ale."

Though I am being totally honest with her about this, what I neglect to mention is that last night, after grabbing a sandwich at the deli, I stopped back at the mini-mart and bought a six-pack of Sam Adams. It currently sits two shy in the fridge. In a fit of guilt and anxiety, I had drinks with dinner to help me cool my nerves while I tried to work through the growing flood of shit I am drowning in.

"Would you believe this isn't the first time I've heard this? You had a slip-up for the first time in fifteen years. It was an accident that was not your fault. I'm sure you've been hyper-fixated on that mistake since, haven't you?"

I nod. "Yes."

"So, with alcohol on the brain and already feeling like you've messed up, your mind played a little trick on you to get you feeling bad again. We've talked about this at length before, how much you have to fight that little feeling inside of you that wants to be miserable. It feels comfortable when you're telling yourself you're a loser, that you're not good enough, right?"

I know what she means all too well. My thoughts have been nothing but guilt over my decision to consciously drink last night. I don't even have to respond.

"So cut yourself a little slack, Mike. Two mistakes is not the same as going out and drinking a whole bottle of tequila. It doesn't undo the hard work you've done to maintain your sobriety for all these years, okay?"

I look down at the trash by my feet, with the two empty Sam Adams bottles, and want to tell her about them. Instead, I keep my mouth shut and nod.

"All right," she says. "Now, let's get to the real root of all this. Let's talk about Brie."

It hurts my heart to hear the name aloud, almost as badly as it did when it came out during my spontaneous writing last night. It was the tipping point which led me to go to the liquor store in the first place.

"First of all, you know what I'm going to say about this Beth business, right?"

"You're going to say it's a coincidence."

"Of course it is. I'm a thousand years old, and I've never even heard of someone named Bitsie before. There's no possible way you could have known her name was Elizabeth when you hired her. It's just a coincidence. Plain and simple. And I don't want you dwelling on it for another second. Understand?"

"Yes."

"I mean it, Mike. Because if you keep on this train of thought, you're going to drive yourself nuts. We've been tiptoeing around this since you got to Seattle, but you know the real reason why you came up with the name Beth, right?"

I shrug, even though I know what she is going to say.

"Because it's similar to Brie, and you've been forcing yourself to avoid confronting what happened to her last time you were at this theater."

"So, what am I supposed to do?"

"I'll tell you what you *shouldn't* do. Don't kill poor Bitsie," she says with a wry smile.

I force a laugh, even though it is becoming a genuine concern. "It's just that the things I write...they're horrible. And they're getting worse."

"The more you try to avoid it, the worse it's going to get. Have you talked to your friend about this? Nate?"

I shake my head. "I haven't talked to anyone. Except you, of course."

"Talk to Nate. Tell him what you're going through. Or if not Nate, then someone. You need to get this off your chest, or it'll follow you around for the rest of your life."

The situation at rehearsal continues to be rough. Alex is refusing to—or perhaps is incapable of—reeling in his performance to match Bitsie. Even worse, it's significantly slowing down the blocking process, and now Bitsie seems to be getting agitated by it. I have never been afraid of my actors before, but what makes things even more complicated is that I am scared of them for completely different reasons.

Everything in my personal and professional life is congealing into one big blob of worry. I pull Nate aside at the beginning of lunch and ask if we can grab some sushi and talk.

"I don't know what to do," I say, putting it bluntly. "I'm treating Alex with kid gloves when it should be Bitsie that I'm worried about. But she's doing great. Her instincts are so spot-on. I just have no notes for her. Meanwhile, it's almost impossible to tell Alex that everything that was previously fine now needs to change. I'm not sure if his ego can handle it."

"You want my honest opinion?" Nate asks.

A pit forms in my stomach, and I wonder if I'm oversharing.

"Depends. Am I going to like it?" I half joke.

"Stop questioning yourself. We already talked about this. You were right before, and you continue to *be* right. I may not be a director, but I've worked enough shows to know this is not a normal situation. Alex is definitely a diva, and talking to him about this is going to be like walking a tightrope over a pit of lions. Pretty much any approach you take could end in disaster."

"Fantastic," I say. "Well, at the very least, I have to thank you for not blaming me for fucking up your play."

"It's not just *my* play, man. That's the whole reason I wanted you to come do this. *Wherever You Go* is for *us*. I wasn't blowing smoke before when I said you're the only one who can do this."

As far as flattery takes me, it still doesn't help fix the issue. "So, what do we do? How do we get this ship back on course?"

Nate sits back in his chair, doing his signature tongue-click when he is mulling something over. "I think you gotta take a page from Jack White. Be like the squirrel girl."

A genuine laugh snorts out of me while memories of the good old days come flooding back. I know the reference he is making.

We used to be obsessed with the White Stripes in our early days together, which is probably why I've had "Seven Nation Army" stuck in my head since my return to Seattle. Back then, whenever one of us was overwhelmed, we would often reference a track from the same album called "Little Acorns."

The song is about the fable of the squirrel trying to gather acorns and store them in a tree for winter. At first, it looks like one insurmountable mountain, but as the intro to the song says, "Once I broke my problems into small pieces, I was able to carry them, just like those acorns, one at a time."

"I take your point," I say. "The question is, which acorn do I start with?"

"Alex is volatile right now. His adjustment to change is harder than Bitsie's. Give him some time. We both agree Bitsie is the new heart of this play. You need to make sure that she's not going to compromise her talent just to make him feel better. This is what you're built for, Mike. You said it yourself. You're not here to make friends. You're here to make a great show. Nurture what's right before it withers on the vine. We'll handle Alex when we need to."

After another half-day of grumbles and sighs, I plan to ask Bitsie to hang back after rehearsal to talk about the Alex problem. To my surprise, she comes to me first, while everyone is packing up. Even though she is already a small woman, she almost shrinks into herself and casts her eyes down as she speaks to me.

"Hey, Mike...I wanted to ask if we could talk and maybe go over a few blocking questions I had?"

For once, I have to fight off a noticeable display of relief instead of anxiety. "That would be great. Do you want to hang back for a minute and we can have the room?"

"Actually..." She twists her toe, digging it into the concrete floor. "I have dinner plans right now. I was wondering if it would be okay to meet up after?"

Something akin to a hiccup quivers in my soul, and that reverberation says "Kill Beth." Hanging around a few minutes after rehearsal is one thing; making plans to meet later is something entirely different. Still, this is the course Nate and I discussed, and God knows I am worried what will happen to the other four bottles of Sam Adams if I just cloister myself away in my apartment for the rest of the night.

"Sure. Want to say around 7:30? Right here?"

"We don't have to come all the way back to the rehearsal space. It's kind of spooky at night. I can just meet you at Greenwood Terrace, if you like."

Alarm bells go off in my head. Though there is nothing in her voice which sounds even the slightest bit flirtatious, it is wildly inappropriate for an actor to invite themselves over to their director's dwelling, alone, at night.

"Let's keep it here. If we're going to work on blocking, it's probably best to keep ourselves oriented with the stage, as we currently have it."

She nods. A smile curls, plumping up her little cheeks. As awkward as it is for her to request to come to my apartment, I feel a tingle in my body that I haven't let myself experience for a long time. It knocks whatever else I had planned to say right out of my head.

Just as quickly as my surge of attraction has come on, an equal and opposite reaction fills the space.

That voice.

Kill Beth.

But this time, it's more than that.

A mental picture wedges its way into my head, one of her sprawled out on the rehearsal room table, with me standing over her. She is moaning, and her clothes are ripped in a dozen places. Blood oozes out of each tear, as if she has been stabbed repeatedly. I envision myself holding a dripping knife.

It takes effort to push the thought away while I excuse myself to grab dinner.

I head to my regular deli and am overcome with a new kind of anxiety as I pick at my plain turkey and cheese sandwich. Butterflies and hurricanes occupy equal parts of my stomach. My life is getting even more confusing.

I have nearly two and a half hours free between rehearsal's end and our meeting, but by the time I have finished my meal, the deli's owner tells me they are closing.

I check my phone. It's already 7:20 p.m.

I know I took my time to eat, worry, and daydream, but I am surprised—and more than a little worried—at just how easily the hours slipped away. This is the second time I have lost track of myself, and it sets my teeth on a musical crusade.

If anything, I am usually *too* punctual. There is an internal clock in me, and the minute hand is made of pure anxiety. I usually check my phone compulsively to make sure I am not late to anything, and yet it has happened again.

What is wrong with me?

<hr>

Even at noon on the brightest day of the year, the rehearsal basement would still be so pitch-black you wouldn't be able to see your hand in front of your face. I make it a point to hurry back and get the lights on to keep it from feeling too "spooky," as Bitsie says.

There is an awkward moment when I first cross the door from the stairwell to the basement, where I am trapped in that infinite darkness, fumbling my hand along the wall for the bank of switches. I slide my hand blindly until I locate them, then flick all three into the upward position with one finger.

Nothing happens.

A blip of panic hits me when I turn them off and back on again.

Still nothing.

Eden always has the lights on before I arrive in the morning. Is there some extra step she takes? Or perhaps there is a power outage in the building?

That's when I see it.

Across the room, there is a single horizontal slice of light sneaking between the bathroom door and the floor. And more than that, a shadow slides across the bottom.

Is someone in there? Maybe there is a breaker in the bathroom to reset the rest of the lights down here and maintenance is working on it. I'm no electrician. All I know is that I am being drawn toward that light.

I pull out my phone and turn on the flashlight. Its dim glow illuminates only a few feet in front of me, and somehow, it makes the surrounding darkness even more ominous. It would almost be safer to fumble around in total darkness rather than having just this one little glimmer of light to fight off such oppressive blackness.

I can't explain it, but there is a strange pressure in my chest when I pass through the door. Even though the lights are on in the bathroom, I am even more creeped out in here than I was in the dark hall.

"Hello?" I call out.

My voice bounces back into my ears, but that is the only reply I get. There are three stall doors, and I have a sudden urge to open each of them to check for intruders. I know I saw something pass through the light. Or at least, I thought I did. I am becoming less sure by the second.

One by one, I push the stall doors. Each time, my heartbeat spikes, and I expect to see some ghoulish figure standing on the toilet, ready to jump out at me. Perhaps Steve the vagrant, holding his knife above his head, prepared to strike.

Every stall is empty, and yet after I have finished my search, my irrational fear is not calmed. I head over to the sink to splash some cold water on my face, when I see something which nearly makes my heart stop.

Neatly folded and placed on the corner of the counter is a brown checkered coat and a folded pair of glasses.

"Chester? Chester, are you here?"

My pulse pounds. I need to be out of this room. But when I throw the door of the bathroom open, someone screams.

The lights are on, and Bitsie is standing in the doorway of the elevator.

"*Ohmygod*, Mike! You scared me!" She clutches at her chest. "What are you doing down here in the dark?"

"I couldn't get the lights to work. And I thought I saw something in the bathroom."

Her mouth tucks into a grin dipped in mischief. "Maybe it was a *ghost*. You know what they say...Every theater is haunted."

I laugh out my nerves, well aware of the superstition and having had more than enough odd encounters over the years to be open to the idea of the supernatural. It is true what she says. Every theater I have ever been to has a story of some ghost haunting the place.

"Maybe you're right," I say. "The ghost of the rehearsal basement."

While on my way to our space, I stop off at the refrigerator to perform my ritual opening and closing.

"Good idea," Bitsie says, assuming I'm grabbing a drink for myself instead of acting on a compulsion.

She peers inside the fridge. "Would you judge me if I grabbed a beer?"

I shake my head. "Oh, we don't have any–"

But I look inside, and my jaw drops. There is a six-pack of Sam Adams sitting in the fridge. Two are missing.

What the actual fuck?

The first thought which leaps into my head is that maybe this place *is* haunted. Either that, or, for completely inexplicable reasons, Chester is going out of his way to mess with my head. I don't have time to have a complete meltdown right now, so I let my teeth tap dance while I reach in and grab her a beer. My hand shifts over to collect a sparkling water, but I watch myself pull out a second Sam Adams instead.

You shouldn't be doing this, Mike. It's all kinds of wrong.
Also, you need to Kill Beth.

I open a drawer and pull out a rusty bottle opener, the kind with a rounded end which hugs the top of the bottle cap while a small, hooked knob catches the underside and yanks it off.

A flash pops into my head, almost like a vision.

I'm holding Bitsie on the ground, my knees straddling her shoulders to keep her pinned. One hand holds her tightly by the throat, and the other uses the bottle opener to pry each tooth from her screaming mouth. She gargles on her own blood. This time, it is much more intense than the intrusive thought I had earlier. I'm not just imagining something. It's like I am there, doing it myself.

Just as soon as the vision came on, I'm right back by the fridge, my hand trembling. I hold the bottle opener against the lip of the beer.

"Everything all right?" Bitsie asks.

"Yeah." I blow out the rest of my breath, as if I am trying to shove all my stress out at once. After opening the drinks, I take a heavy pull on mine to calm my nerves, simultaneously kicking myself for continuing to make poor choices. "Just do me a favor and don't mention the beer to Nate. I don't think it would make him too happy."

Bitsie gives me a look of slight confusion but quickly shrugs it off. "I won't say anything if you don't."

A smile comes to me easier than I expect, given what has just happened. "All right, then. Let's head inside."

"While we're on the topic of things kept just between us, do you mind if I ask something about the cast? Or, more specifically, about Alex?"

I knew this was coming. Or, at least, I was hoping it would be. "Anything."

"Was he really close with Cassandra or something? I know we kind of got off on the wrong foot, but I was hoping he'd lighten up at some point."

I twist my mouth to the side, considering her question. "Honestly, not really. They had good stage chemistry, but as far as I know, they weren't overly friendly outside of rehearsal. They ran lines occasionally after work, but that's pretty much the extent of it."

"In that case, I don't know how to put this...Am I doing something wrong? Every time I open my mouth, I get this feeling like he hates me."

I nod, not because I agree, but because I understand where she is coming from. "I think Alex is in a delicate place right now. I'm sure you know about him recently losing his brother on that haunted house show, and he's trying to live up to the legacy of his father. When he signed onto the project, he was front and center. And when we were doing our table reads and blocking Act 1, I think Cassandra approached her performance in a purely reactive manner, following his lead every step of the way."

"I can do that if you want. It's just that you never gave me any notes otherwise, so I've been playing the character the same way I did during my audition."

"That's where things get a little tricky. Again, we're in a cone of silence here. After seeing your audition, Nate and I agreed that your performance was kind of a game changer. It made us re-evaluate the whole way Husband and Wife's relationship should be portrayed."

Again, she looks at me like she is not quite understanding what I am saying. I decide to lay my cards on the table and put it all out in simple terms.

"The Wife was initially written to be the real main character, but when we got such a big name as Alex Keating onboard, the attention shifted to him. Now that you're here and I've seen how intuitively and perfectly you can bring Wife to life, it's time to go back to the original vision and put you at the forefront. And to be completely frank, Alex is going to need to find a way to suck it up and deal with that."

Bitsie sips her beer and nods. Her eyes are big and glassy while she absorbs the weight of the comment—that a small-time local actress is upstaging such a major talent.

"Thank you for giving me this chance," she says. "But that still leaves the question, what do I do about Alex?"

This time, it's my turn to take another sip while I think through the best way to answer.

"First off, I don't want you to let him intimidate you into changing your performance. I'm the one in charge, and this is what's happening. But if it's not too much to ask, maybe you could invite him out to lunch or dinner to clear the air? I think it would go a long way if it seemed like it came from you. Don't even bring up the play or performances or any of that stuff. Just get to know him, and maybe that'll soften him up a bit?"

She nods. "Okay. I can do that. I really love this script. Honestly, I feel like this show could be really special. I just want to make sure we get it right."

"Me too!" I chuckle. The beer is starting to go to my head. A question pops into my mind, and I can't help but blurt it out. "What is it about the play that draws you to it?"

"Honestly, I was hooked from the title alone. When I was a kid, I used to hear that phrase a lot. *Wherever you go, there you are.* I didn't know what it meant until I got older. To be completely honest, I haven't had the easiest life. I mean, who has?" She pauses for an awkward laugh. "But as time's gone on, I feel like that phrase has almost become a thesis statement for my whole life. It really resonated with me, and I think the sentiment is conveyed brilliantly in the way the story's told." Her big blue eyes cut into me. "What about you?"

I don't know why, but there is something about this moment that feels raw and perfect. Though I haven't told the story about Brie to anyone other than Nate, who experienced it with me, and Dr. Jules, I open my mouth, ready to spill it all.

The sound of a door slamming shut somewhere in the basement nearly makes me jump out of my skin.

"Jesus," I say, hopping off the table and heading out into the common area. "Hello?"

There is no movement, no reply, no doors opened or closed. Everything is just as it was.

"That was weird," I say, coming back into our rehearsal room.

"I told you. Ghosts," she says.

"Must be. Anyways, we should get to work. What scene did you want to start with?"

Once we finish rehearsing, I tell Bitsie to head on home without me, that I need to clean up and use the restroom. After the door to the elevator closes, I count to ten before I toss the empty bottles in the trash, then head to the fridge and pull out the remaining two beers. I open one and slug the whole thing back in a long chug, then tuck the last into my bag.

Tonight has been confusing and frightening enough. As much as I hate to admit it, the alcohol helps keep the unwanted, intrusive thoughts at bay.

"This is helping." I say the words out loud to try and convince myself, though having my words reverberate back into me makes them sound like a false, almost mocking gesture.

Before I go, I head into the bathroom to retrieve Chester's coat and glasses for him, only to find them missing. A story forms in my head, one of Chester realizing he has left his things in the basement, then coming down to retrieve them while Bitsie and I were rehearsing. It would explain the sudden slamming of the door.

The opportunity to ask him about it presents itself while I climb the stairs at Greenwood Terrace. He is smoking on the balcony in front of his room.

"Evening, Mike," he says, nodding to me. "Feeling better?"

For a second, I don't know what he is talking about.

Oh. He caught me being ill in the bathroom yesterday.

"Yeah. Listen, this may sound like a weird question…Were you in the rehearsal basement tonight?"

"Tonight?" He raises his eyebrows at me. "Can't say that I was."

"You sure?" I press, knowing for certain they were his coat and glasses. It is the very same set he is wearing right now.

"Why would I lie?" He takes a long drag on his smoke. "I took the family out for a nice dinner at an Italian restaurant uptown.

I don't know why, but I feel an uncontrollable urge to keep pushing. "Are they in your room right now? I'd love to say hello."

"Would you believe that, for once, they're actually asleep at a reasonable hour? It's a small miracle. Though I'm sure they'll be back up by three in the morning, shaking me awake to play games or watch the telly."

"Maybe I can meet them another night, then."

"Of course. Maybe one of these days we can all grab a bite together." He stubs his cigarette out on the rail and drops it to his feet. "Anyway, I should probably turn in for the night myself."

He pivots to open his door, and I head over to do the same.

"Oh, but that reminds me…Don't forget to *Kill Beth*."

His words stop me cold.

"What did you say?"

"You heard me, Mikey boy. Before this is all over, you've got to kill Beth. It's only right, chum."

"What the fuck are you talking about? Have you been in my apartment?"

"Sleep well, Mike. I'll be seeing you."

He winks at me, then pushes his door open.

I make a move, grabbing him by the shoulder. My hand slips off when I catch the briefest glimpse inside his unit.

A blond woman lies in bed, surrounded by a pool of blood so large there is more red than white. Her eyes are wide open, as is her mouth.

The walls are painted in arterial streaks. On the floor is a young boy who is nothing more than a heap of twisted limbs. His dinosaur-printed pajamas are similarly covered in blood, and there is a deep red stain set into the rug.

I only see it for half a second before Chester enters his room and closes the door in my face. When I rush forward and twist the knob. It's locked.

I take a step over to the window and try to peer through the shades, seeing only darkness where there was light just a moment ago. With a shaking hand, I grab my phone and turn on the flashlight app, then press it against the glass.

Nothing but an empty apartment.

I pound my fist against the window. "Chester! Chester, open the door!" I shout.

I continue to beat my hand against the glass until a disgruntled voice calls out from beneath me. It's Elaine.

"Mike, can you keep it down? I'm trying to go to bed."

I stagger back until my body presses against the rail. My phone drops from my hand. When I bend over to pick it up, I notice one last thing.

The cigarette butt Chester just dropped.

It's gone.

Or maybe it was never there.

Spontaneous Writing: Session 8

You're losing it, Mikey old boy
This isnt a game
This isnt a toy
You've finally gone and taken the plunge
Lock you up for what you've done
Have a tequila, with some lime
Perfect way to lose some time,
Carrots and Brie, Carrots and Brie
Drag Beth out for all to see
Write your words with blade on skin
It's a spontaneous writing win
Carve your name into her chest
Imbue her with your family crest
You've already murdered once before
But it's been so long, you're such a bore
Do it for me, won't you please?
Do it for my family
Caleb, Susie, Chester too
The time has come to pay your dues
You think you've lost it, gone insane

But let me make this very plain
Everything's according to plan
So let me be your guiding hand
Heed the words I say to thee
Carrots and Brie, carrots and Brie

CHAPTER 8

I texted Nate late last night and said I needed to speak with him. He probably thinks I just want to go over my meeting with Bitsie. But after what I saw in Chester's apartment, I don't know who else to turn to. Even if Nate thinks I am going insane, I can't keep this bottled up anymore.

He agreed to have breakfast with me this morning. I don't want to be alone with myself, even for a minute, unable to trust what I will do without supervision. It is such an overwhelming worry for me that I asked Nate to come to Greenwood Terrace so we can walk together. I have experienced missing hours multiple times now, potential hallucinations, intrusive obsessive thoughts, and I don't even know what else.

When I step outside, I hope to see Nate already standing there, but he is running late. In the meantime, I cannot help myself. Once again, I try to peer through Chester's window, through the small slit in the curtains. I'm able to make out the shapes of a bed, a side table, a couch.

All empty.

A sharp pain pricks the back of the hand cupped against the glass, and I flail when I notice the fat body of a black spider perched on it. I smack it off with my other hand. The spider swings on a strand of web attached to the top sill of the window and lands on the wooden siding of the building. It quickly skitters into a gap in one of the many boards.

A shiver runs through me, and I take another step back. A centipede speeds out from the hole, cuts a line across the wood, and tucks into another gap in the slats.

"You good?" Nate's voice from behind makes me jump.

"Goddamn spider just bit me." I show him the quickly swelling red spot on the back of my hand. It burns and itches at the same time, inviting me to scratch at the searing pain. "I hope it's not black widow or a brown recluse."

"Nah, we don't have those up here. Too cold. You'll be fine."

"Fine is the last word I would use to describe me right now," I say, unable to stop myself from scraping my nails around the red bump.

Nate starts to head down the stairs. "Come on. Let's grab something to eat and you can tell me about it. What's going on?"

"Um...I'll tell you in a minute." I look around at the other apartments while we make our way to the street, too afraid to say anything out loud until we have managed some distance. These walls are thin, and I don't want to broadcast my potential insanity to my actors.

"You're freaking me out, Mike. What is it?" Nate asks once we are on the sidewalk.

"I don't even know how to say it. I think I might be losing my mind. Or...I don't know...I'm being haunted?" I wince, ready for Nate's already serious face to grow dark and stretch into a concerned frown. Instead, I earn a look of casual recognition.

"Oh, you mean Chester?"

My eyes go so wide it feels like they are about to pop out of my head. "How did you know?"

Nate presses his lips together and makes a sound like a deflating balloon. "*Everybody* knows about Chester. This place is haunted as fuck."

"I'm sorry. This is coming as a bit of a shock," I say. We round the corner and enter a small bakery. I nearly collapse into a chair after grabbing my morning latte and muffin from the front. "You're saying you *actually* believe in ghosts?"

"Come on, man. It's the theater. Of course it's haunted. What's he done? Shifting shadows? Spooky sounds? Moving stuff around?"

"Yes! I mean, yeah." I try to compose myself in the face of such absolute validation. "All of that and more. I keep seeing him in the middle of the night outside my room.

"Damn, dude. You've actually seen him in person? Now, that's rare."

"*Seen* him? I've had full-on conversations with him. Last night, as he walked back into his apartment, I could have sworn I saw the bodies of a woman and kid *dead* inside the apartment next to me."

Finally, I get the reaction I am looking for.

Nate's mouth drops a little, and his eyes flash in surprise. "Does this happen to you a lot? Like, have you seen other ghosts at other theaters?" He leans in. "Are you a ghost whisperer?"

"No, never! It's not that I don't believe in the paranormal, and of course, you hear weird stuff. But that's usually just people jumping to conclusions when a C-clamped light creaks on a catwalk or pre-programmed sound cues go off out of sequence. What's happening here is on a *whole* different level. I'll be honest...It's really freaking me out."

I wasn't going to show Nate this, but now that he is so fully onboard, it doesn't seem quite as insane. So, I pull out my laptop and open a document. "I've been doing this thing with my therapist called spontaneous writing. The idea is that I totally clear my head of all thoughts and just let my hands write whatever they're going to write. I had been so anxious about coming back here...she thought it could be a good exercise to, I don't know, get in touch with myself or something."

Nate spends a minute reading through each of the eight entries. "Shiiiiiit," he says after an agonizing amount of time. "This is some pretty messed-up stuff. So...what? You think he's, like, possessing you or something to write all of this?"

"I don't know. I don't understand any of it."

"Damn. I forgot his kid's name was Caleb. You've got it all down here."

Another shock to my system. "You knew his name?"

Realization dawns on Nate, and he rubs his hands down his face. "Oh, man. You don't even remember the story, do you?"

I shake my head. "No!"

"I know we got pretty loaded back in the day, but you can't tell me you've forgotten the story. We used to talk about it all the time. *Everyone* did."

Something flashes in my head. Just a tiny spark of a memory, but that is all. "I must have blocked it out. Remind me."

"Okay." Nate shakes out his hands and rolls his shoulders back to get himself into storyteller mode. "So, like, twenty years ago, before we even started working at The Burgess, there was this director named Chester...something or other. I forget his last name. He was foreign, I think—"

"British," I say.

Nate snaps his fingers. "Yeah. So, when he came to town, he brought his whole family with him. And while he was working, his family got bored, especially the kid, Caleb. He made friends with some local children, one of whom ended up being kinda fucked in the head. One day, Chester comes home from rehearsal and finds his wife and son murdered. He calls the cops, and according to the story, he mentions seeing the kid come out from the closet or bathroom, holding a knife. And then he, like...got killed while still on the call. They never figured it out."

While Nate tells the story, long-dead synapses reconnect, and I start to remember the details. "Oh my god. I *do* remember."

"Okay, so, hear me out...And I'm not saying it's not really Chester because, damn. Dude...Even I've had encounters I can't explain. But what if you've been stressing so much about coming back here, thinking about what happened to Brie, that you've sort of conjured up the ghost of Chester? Like some latent memory type shit that's rising to the surface because of past trauma? I mean, you mention her in your writing, so you obviously have her on your mind. That, along with whoever this Beth is...Who is Beth, by the way?"

"My therapist thinks I made her up, just coming up with a name that sounds like Brie. But my crazy-person theory is that Beth is *Bitsie*. You know, since her real name is Elizabeth?"

Nate bursts into genuine laughter. "Oh man. No wonder you

freaked out on her first day!" Another thought pops into his head, and he slaps the table several times with excitement. "Oh man! Get this! So they say the killer was a kid, right? What if the kid's name was Beth, and this whole time, Chester's been trying to convince you to get vengeance for their deaths?"

At this point, Nate has gone so far down the rabbit hole that I cannot tell if he is pulling my leg. The part that scares me is it makes a lot of sense. "Do *you* think that Bitsie is Beth?"

Nate laughs again. "Of course not! Look, man. I don't know how much of this is haunting and how much is your brain messing with you. If you ask me, it's probably a little bit of both. My guess is you probably cooked up Beth because there's, like, fifteen Elizabeths on the wall, and you just latched onto it."

"Wait." I put my hand up. "What do you mean by 'the wall?'"

"You know, in the rehearsal hall. Come on. Let's go count them. It's time to head over anyway."

I feel like I'm unable to take another breath until we are four flights underground and standing in the common area of the rehearsal basement. Nate points to nearly a hundred framed headshots forming a huge grid along the wall by the fridge, each with a name underneath.

"Rebecca Burgess used to love doing this back in the day—for local talent, out of towners, anyone she liked, really. Here, let's count."

We scan the pictures, one of which features Bitsie's headshot using her full name underneath. It is located right next to where I have to open and shut the fridge every time I pass through the space.

"I count twelve Elizabeths. I bet you've been subconsciously looking at these every day, and it just sort of sunk into your brain." Nate then jumps, exclaiming while he points to one picture. "Oh! Here's Chester! Look! Chester Mays. This is the guy, right?"

"Holy shit. There he is."

Next to the door to our rehearsal hall, sitting on the far left, is Chester. He is even wearing the same checkered coat and glasses.

"This explains so much. Maybe I'm not totally crazy after all."

"Well, you're a *little* crazy. But who in the theater world isn't? At least now you've got something plausible to fall back on."

"Mike?" Eden calls out from the rehearsal room. "What are you going on about?"

"I'm just looking at the wall," I say when she rounds the corner to join us. "Do you know the story of Chester Mays?"

Eden snorts. "Of course. Who doesn't?"

———

Through brute force, we manage to finish blocking the play by the end of the morning. On my advice, Bitsie invites Alex out to lunch. I can't say that it improves his demeanor when we start basically re-blocking Act 1 in the afternoon, but we make it through the day without any hissy fits, which I call a win.

Also, my fear of Bitsie has greatly diminished. As weird as it is to try to rationalize, I feel some degree of comfort in asserting to myself that, instead of going insane, I'm actually being haunted. And as such, it helps me justify some of the other strange things happening in my life.

If there is a ghost living next door, he must have been the one messing around with my papers when I was out. He is the one typing those horrible things during my spontaneous writing sessions. And for all I know, it could have been the ghost who shattered the glass in front of the fireplace.

Much like when I received my obsessive-compulsive diagnosis, it helps me find peace of mind to have some idea of what is going on. Of course, I am still terrified of what I will see when I get home tonight, still worried about the things Chester will do to try and make me lose my mind, and still very concerned about my bouts of lost time, but at least I am not afraid of whether I am slowly having a stroke or an aneurysm. After fifteen years of directing shows all over the country, having count-less inexplicable moments, and hearing more paranormal stories than I can possibly remember, I have never been so ready to accept that ghosts are very real.

Now I just need to figure out how to deal with mine.

After ending rehearsal for the day, I treat myself to a nice dinner at a local seafood restaurant and take my time before making the walk back home. Of course, while I count the stairs up to Greenwood Terrace, a familiar face greets me at the top level.

"Aren't you looking positively chuffed..." Chester blows a huge puff of cigarette smoke in my face.

"I'm not afraid of you," I say, though the compulsive scratching at the spider bite on my hand and slight quaver to my voice argues otherwise.

"Oh really?" he asks with a dark grin. "Let's see what we can do about that."

He grabs me by the wrist and plunges the burning cherry of his cigarette into my spider bite. The pain is excruciating. He may be a ghost, but that doesn't make him any less real. I grit my teeth, shut my eyes, and hiss in pain as I am driven to my knees.

"Look at it," he says, but I refuse. Chester grips my wrist harder, like he is about to crush my bones. "I said, look at it!"

The pain extends into my head. His words drive into my ears like a hammer and chisel. My eyes flutter open. There is a burn so deep in the back of my hand that I swear I can see bone.

I look up at his face, and my breath catches in my throat.

Rivers of blood run from his eyes. His mouth is open, presenting black, decayed teeth inside a rotten mouth. Spiders, centipedes, and cockroaches crawl out from it, and a dozen flies encircle his head.

He finally releases his grip on my wrist. I fall to my hands and knees.

"Just because you think you know who you're dealing with, it won't bring you any closer to being rid of me. I *own* you, Mikey boy. I know what you've done. And believe me, before I'm finished, you *will* kill Beth."

I crawl past Chester, yanking my keys from my pocket and fumbling to get them into the door as fast as possible. He cackles while I do; each syllable of his laughter is a hammer pounding the spikes deeper into my brain. When I slam the door behind me, there is an immediate relief of the pressure in my head.

I clamor to my feet, cursing at myself and my stupid compulsions while I check the fridge and stove. Then I rush over to the sink to put cold water on the burn.

No more than two seconds have passed when there is a knock at my door. Chester is not finished with me, and he has already shown me what happens when I disobey.

Every nerve in my body tightens. Any relief I felt earlier has evaporated. Chester is so much worse as a reality than a figment of my imagination. Whatever it is he has in store for me, it is better to just get it over with than to test his limits. I rip the door open, and my legs nearly give out on me.

It's Bitsie. She has changed from her oversized rehearsal sweats into a tight-fitting shirt and black leggings. In her hand is a mostly full bottle of Merlot.

"Hey, Mike. You okay?"

"Yeah, I…" I glance down at my hand. The burn is gone. All that remains is the spider bite, red and swollen, but nothing like what was there before. The pain has also receded, down to the mild itching burn I have felt all day. "I just got a spider bite on my way up the stairs."

"Oh my gosh," she says, stepping inside. "That looks painful."

"I'll be all right. What are you doing here?"

"I was hanging out with Danny and heard you shout. I was worried. You mind if I come in?"

I want to say no, that it is inappropriate, but I'm terrified of what Chester will do if I am left alone.

I back away from the door, welcoming her into my meticulously clean apartment. She crosses over to the kitchenette and grabs a pair of stemmed glasses.

"You want some wine?" she asks.

I'm about to say no, but she has already filled both. Instead of answering, I grab the glass and have a sip.

It's been nearly two decades since I've had wine. The drink is richer than I remember, more decadent. Another wave of guilt assults me, not just for slipping up again, but for how easy it is becoming to give in.

Bitsie sinks onto the couch. I feel awkward standing, but the only other chair in the room is tucked into my work nook, so I sit next to her.

"I saw you went to lunch with Alex. How did it go?" I ask.

She takes a deep sip, and so do I. I need something to slow my heart after my encounter with Chester. And almost at an equal level, I need to calm my racing pulse at having this beautiful woman so close to me in my room.

"I wish I could say it went better. I didn't bring up the show, like you said. But he did. He more or less told me where we stand and where I can shove it if I think I'm going to upstage him."

"Oh, hell," I say, taking another swig. "I'll talk to him tomorrow, see what I can do to get him onboard. We're already so far behind. It'll be a small miracle if we have something presentable in time for previews."

"I'm sorry I've messed things up so badly." Bitsie lowers her big eyes to the floor.

"No," I reassure her. "I already told you it's not your fault. Jesus...I feel like a monster saying this, but having you come in has been one of the best things to happen to the show."

"You really mean it?"

"Yeah, I do."

I go to take another sip of my wine, but the glass is already empty. Without me saying a word, Bitsie refills it. The alcohol is already going to my head. The wine is strong. It hits me differently than beer, makes me feel warm.

"You asked me yesterday what drew me to this play," she says. "I've been meaning to ask, what drove you to write it?"

I shake my head. "Well, Nate wrote it, not me. But he did fight pretty hard to get me to come here and direct it. He said I was the only one that could do it...because of our history together."

"Why? What happened?" She looks up at me, her eyes filled with curiosity. Even sitting down, it's no wonder she goes by Bitsie; I'm almost a head taller than her.

"It's a story that's not particularly flattering," I say.

"In my experience, the truth behind most art isn't. But finding a way to harness the ugly moments in life and shape them into something meaningful is how you find the beauty."

I sigh and take another sip of wine, unable to believe I am about to tell her the story.

"Fifteen years ago, I was directing my first play. It was here, at The Burgess. Nate Mulligan and I were best friends, having worked as crew for a bunch of shows beforehand. We also used to party pretty hard.

Drinking, drugs...Most nights after a show, we wouldn't be in bed until after the sun was up. Sometimes, we'd go so hard that we'd forgo sleep altogether, and it wouldn't be until the next night after another show that we'd finally crash out.

"Despite all this, we still got our work done, so we didn't think there was a problem. Rebecca Burgess believed in me enough to hand me the reins to direct my first play. It was a production of *Cyrano*. Because I was a newbie, I begged Rebecca to let Nate come on as an Assistant Stage Manager. I don't mean this as an excuse, but as much of a shitshow of a person as I was, he was one hell of an enabler. When you put the two of us together, it was like we cranked things up to an entirely different level.

"And because we were more or less the same age as the cast and I didn't have any concept of boundaries at the time, we would invite them out with us at night. There was this one girl, Brie. She was actually Nate's sister, believe it or not. She was playing Roxane. No nepotism, I swear. They were just a theater family, and her talent was..."

A swell of emotion rises in me. My vision grows blurry. My mouth is dry, and I remedy it with another big gulp of wine.

"Brie was incredibly gifted. And she wasn't caught up in all the shit me and Nate were, at least not until *Cyrano*. She started going out with us after rehearsal. And at first, it was great. We would party 'til six, crash for two hours, then get up, go to work, and do it all over again. That was, until this one night.

"We'd been drinking hard—like, each had a full bottle of tequila hard—and up until that point, she'd never tried any drugs harder than pot. We were supposed to start tech the next day, which, you know, is brutal. But it's not like you're actually doing much acting during tech, you know? Especially for the first couple days...You're mostly just a walking puppet for eight hours so lighting can get their cues down. So, I got the bright idea to choose that night of *all* nights to introduce her to ecstasy. Because, screw it, she doesn't even really need to act tomorrow.

"We started at Shakespeare's Head with some drinks, then headed to a nearby club. I have no idea when we got back to these apartments. I want to say around three? Everything was going fine, and then *bam*, she's on the ground, just shaking and foaming at the mouth. It was a seizure.

"Nate and I were terrified. Neither of us had any idea what to do. Hell, we were blasted out of our minds ourselves. We called 911, but by the time the paramedics arrived, she was already gone. It was horrible, watching her die and knowing we couldn't do anything about it.

"Afterward, I was a wreck. I felt responsible. I *still* feel responsible. Nate and I swore to sobriety, something I've kept up until...well, until very recently, actually. And as much of a mess as I was, Nate..."

I shake my head. His story isn't mine to tell.

"Anyway, I've distanced myself from my cast ever since. And I never came back to Seattle again. But you know the saying...wherever you go, there you are. And it's so true. Everywhere I went, I saw her face. Every time a cast member invited me out, it was all I could think about. I just shut myself down and focused on work. I've always had OCD to some degree, but after that, it just went into overdrive. And that's been my life for fifteen years. Just work and trying to forget. But I guess you can only outrun yourself for so long. Nate must have figured that out before me because, well, here I am. And then I met you and—"

Bitsie puts her warm hands on my face. My cheeks are wet. I didn't even realize I'm crying. It is the closest human contact I've had in forever, and I am putty in her palms when she pulls me in and kisses me.

Her lips are so soft, so comforting. I want to pull away—at least, that is what I try to tell myself. But it's a lie. I want this more than anything I have wanted in my adult life. I just poured my heart out, shared my darkest truth, and instead of recoiling in horror, Bitsie is pulling me in, kissing me hard. She presses her body against mine. I can feel every bit of it when I wrap my arms around her and pull her even tighter, not wanting her to ever let go.

Fifteen years of abstinence from life all comes crashing down in a flood of affection and acceptance. She pulls at my shirt; I pull at hers. Our lips break, only to be rid of our clothes so that there is nothing left between us. Her body is on fire, and so is mine. There is no OCD, no Chester, no Nate, no show, no Beth. There's only this moment, right here, and us in the middle of it.

Finally, she pulls away, and my heart breaks. I worry the moment has passed. Instead, she grabs me by the hand, pulls me up, and leads me toward the bed.

"Come on," she says, then draws me closer for another kiss.

I try to say something, but I don't even know what it is. It just comes out as a moan of desire. The next thing I know, we are fully cradled in each other. Our pants are gone, but I don't even know how. We're closer, closer...

This is everything.

She is everything.

<hr />

I wake up slowly. My head is gently pounding. The room is swimming behind my eyes. I wait for regret to seep in while I creep back into consciousness, but it doesn't come. No fear, no anxiety...The only thing I feel is cold. I'm naked, and a shiver runs through me from the chill coming in from an open window. For the first time since I was young, I roll over to cuddle into a warm body next to me.

Instead, my arm wraps around something cold and wet.

My eyes fly open. All I see is porcelain white hidden under a mess of hair soaked in blood. I scream, pulling myself back.

Her eyes stare blankly at the ceiling. Her throat is slit, a wide gash, and severed tendons fray out of the hole like a cut rope. I rise to my feet, my body trembling. Blood covers half my torso—sticky, wet, and freezing cold.

On the couch, framed against the window, sits Chester, merely a silhouette save for his white eyes and gleaming teeth behind a wicked grin.

"Was it good for you too?" he asks, soaking up my terror with pure glee.

My head spins, and I fall to my knees. There is something else between me and him, on the floor. A heap of arms and legs. Small, like a child.

I look back at Bitsie in the bed, but something is not right. It doesn't look like Bitsie. Her hair, matted to her face, is blond instead of a dark brunette. It's too long, too tangled. And her face is the wrong shape.

Knowledge from some unknown places are shoved into my awareness. I'm staring at Chester's murdered wife.

I scream again and find myself transported back into bed. Chester is gone, and so is the boy. An arm wraps around my bare chest.

It's Bitsie, her eyes glowing bright blue in the darkness.

"Mike, are you okay?"

Spontaneous Writing: Session 9

Mikey boy, what are you to do?
Now you've gone and screwed the pooch
You think she's not THE actual Beth?
The one who killed me and the rest?
I've got news for you son,
More will be dead before this is done
You're willpower's seeming spotty too
I thought you quit the drugs and booze?
And what about that missing time?
You sure you haven't done more crime?
I'm in your head, you can't get free
Carrots and Brie, Carrots and Brie
And speaking of which, you spilled the beans
You think that makes your conscience clean?
Brie is dead, while you still live
You can't forget, I won't forgive
What would Nate say if he discovered
The things you're hiding from her brother
You haven't told him about the booze
I wonder how he'll take the news?

Carrots and Brie, carrots and Brie
I dare you to try and ignore me
I'm in your blood, I'm in your hands
I'm in your head making new plans
And now you'll pay the Devil's due
When you find out what's in store for you.

CHAPTER 9

In my dream last night, when first I thought I was awake, I had this overwhelming sense of calm and peace—a feeling of relief and contentment after sleeping with Bitsie.

That is all gone now that the harsh morning sun cuts into my apartment.

Regret floods into me from all directions. Not just for the intimacy —which, of course, is highly inappropriate. More for sharing my story about Brie. I barely know this woman. Hell, it took nearly six months of working with Dr. Jules before I was comfortable enough to confide in her. And even then, it was like pulling teeth.

I look at the perfect, warm woman still nuzzled next to me, and every time I blink, all I picture is the face of Chester's wife, her throat exposed, those big blue eyes a dead gray, staring forever at the ceiling. And after last night's encounter with Chester, I have a deep, unshakable dread that he is going to do something to Bitsie. Somehow, he will find a way.

Even more than that, I am now totally convinced he was the one responsible for Cassandra's injury, that it was his spectral hand which guided Bitsie to where she is now.

A new worm of a thought crawls into my ear.

Why go through all this trouble if she isn't the real Beth? Why torment me, make me feel like I'm going crazy, if it is not all part of some grand scheme to lure his family's killer into a position where Chester can finally get his revenge?

But then, there is another side of me, one which is so grateful to Bitsie. The woman who trusted me, was vulnerable with me, and didn't judge me for admitting my life's biggest regret. How could this small, empathetic woman possibly be a killer?

I slowly climb out of bed, trying not to disturb her. My blood runs cold when I notice my laptop sitting open. There is a new spontaneous writing session sitting on the screen, only I have no memory of writing it. It's impossible for me to believe this is all just the result of my psyche manifesting itself in bizarre ways.

It's Chester. It's *all* Chester. It has to be.

"What's that?" Bitsie's voice is groggy with vocal fry when she leans over my shoulder and wraps her arms around my neck.

I don't know whether to pull her in tighter or throw her off me.

"Just some notes for how to deal with Alex," I say. "I think there's no way around it. I'm going to have to confront him today. I just need to find the right way to phrase it."

"I'm sure you'll do great." Her hot breath melts my ear as she speaks. Her hair tickles while it glides across my neck. She kisses me on the cheek. A ripple of cold is left behind when she pulls away and gets dressed.

I squeeze my eyes shut. Words I don't want to say bubble up from my gut. "Does the name *Chester Mays* mean anything to you?"

She stops midway through pulling up her black leggings. Her eyes narrow, and she appears to drift off to someplace else. After a few seconds, Bitsie shakes her head. "Nope. Should it?"

I get up and close my laptop. "It's stupid. Remember the other night when we were in the rehearsal hall, joking about ghosts? I heard this story about a director from years ago that got murdered here. Apparently, he's a bit of a legend around The Burgess. Since you're local, I was just curious if you'd heard of him."

The corners of her lips pull down, not necessarily a frown. More like a display of a regretful lack of insight. "Sorry, must have been before my time. Though I do love a good ghost story."

The alarm on my phone goes off, signaling it is time to leave.

Bitsie grabs it since she is closer to the bed. She turns it off and tosses it to me. "Maybe you can tell it to me tonight. I think it's best if I make a swift exit for now." She gives me a conspiratorial wink, then pulls her shirt on. "I'm guessing this doesn't really need to be said, but we definitely shouldn't mention this to anyone else, right?"

I am trying to process three things at once, but a hangover blends them all in my head.

No, we definitely *shouldn't* tell anyone about our sexual indiscretion. Additionally, the way she mentioned talking more tonight gives me pause. As much as I needed this and as deeply as I want to do this again, I don't think it is a good idea. Not for us or in the best interest of the show. And finally, there is an unsettling feeling, like she just lied to me when she said she didn't know anything about Chester.

Before I have a chance to follow up on any of these points, she slips out my door and sneaks down the stairs of the complex.

"Hey, Alex? Can we talk?" I pull him aside at the beginning of lunch.

We have been able to make it most of the way through Act 1 in our re-blocking run-through, and the further we get, the more adversarial he becomes. Even the moments where he used to show affection to the Wife character now feel cold and petty.

"It's about goddamn time." Alex pulls up a chair. "I was starting to think you'd forgotten about me."

I sit on the edge of a table. It feels awkward, like I am trying to be the *cool* teacher in a high school. I keep my voice down since the rest of the cast is just outside the rehearsal room, preparing their lunches.

"I'm sorry that you feel neglected. I probably should have talked to you sooner, and that's my fault. Part of me was hoping that you and Bitsie would be able to work things out on your own, without me having to interfere. I understand you two had a talk yesterday that may not have gone so well."

"I thought it did. I said what I had to. It's not my fault if she didn't get the message."

Even though I know what he is going to say, I try to make sure he feels heard. "And what message is that?"

"That she can't just come in here and fuck up everything we've already built. It's not only disrespectful to me; it's disrespectful to all the work Cassandra put in that went straight out the window the second Bitsie came in. And here you are, just letting her walk all over you and get away with it. Somebody had to say something."

I try to mask a sigh. Thankfully, this isn't the first time I've needed to have a difficult conversation regarding an actor's behavior. I have my response already tucked up my sleeve.

"You know, I've worked with a lot of different actors, and everyone has their own style. One thing that happens from time to time, especially in shows that have as much confrontation as this one, is that performers start to look at each scene almost as if it were a boxing match. It's like each fight on the stage needs to be approached as if it were a fight in real life. But the problem with that mentality is that it sort of has a way of taking over your whole headspace. Every scene, every interaction, becomes a new bout, and instead of *listening* to each other, you're fighting to get your half of the story told. It just doesn't work.

"The way I like to look at it is more like you're dancing partners. Every moment is a step you take together, a choreography of movement and emotion that can be beautiful, whether it's slow and intimate or fast and violent. When you're dancing, you're connected and communicating in a way that goes beyond the words on the page. You're not stepping on anybody's toes because you're in this *together*."

Alex nods, though he seems primed to strike back. "Yeah, but every dance has someone who leads and someone who follows. I'm the leader. I've been the leader this whole time. It doesn't work when you have a partner who refuses to follow."

I nod, understanding his point and hoping the metaphor doesn't get muddled with my response. "That's true, but it's a give-and-take. There isn't just one leader. You need to take turns...Find a middle ground...How about the three of us sit down this afternoon, go through the script scene by scene, find out who is the best leader for each? And then come to a compromise to trust that your co-star will guide the tone in a way that brings out the best in both of you?"

Alex's knuckles pop, and he throws himself to his feet. "Are you forgetting *who* I am? I'm a goddamned Keating! I know how to lead. I did it the whole time Cassandra was here, and you were fine with it until Bitsie showed up. *I'm* the star here. You think people are paying to come see some nobody play a sad, weepy bitch the whole play? They want conflict! They want to see a marriage that *is* a boxing match. They want to see *me*!"

My face is hot. My head throbs and eyes burn. I shut them tightly and rub my hands against my temples. Instead of calming, an uncontrollable rage boils over me. I rise to my feet, meeting him face-to-face, and allow my tone to match his.

"You think this whole show is about you? Well, I've got news for you, buddy...You're not your brother, and you *certainly* aren't your father. Just because your last name is Keating doesn't automatically give you the right to steamroll *my* show. *I'm* the director, and when you're on my stage, you will do as I say because *I'm* the one with the vision. *I'm* the one who understands whether the audience is going to see you as a troubled husband or whiny little brat who's too self-centered to be able to get out of his own way because he can't handle risking a woman with more talent than him upstaging him for even a second.

"Yes, the tone of the show has changed because the *people* in it have changed. The level of talent in our cast has changed, and you're going to need to find a way to put your ego in check long enough to realize that there are *two* stars in this show. And if you listen to either of us for a goddamn second, you might realize that maybe, by listening instead of fighting every second of the day, you might learn something. You may even find a way for your own performance to grow and become something better than a pitiful little man throwing a hissy fit on stage."

Alex turns from me and bursts into the common room like a runaway boulder. "Sure, sure. Big words coming from the man who's fucking the co-star!" He throws an accusatory finger at Bitsie for good measure.

My face grows even hotter, but this time, it is from embarrassment instead of rage.

"Oh? You don't think everyone heard you two banging last night in your room? News flash, asshole...While you were busy screwing, me and Elaine were sharing a drink out on the front patio. We heard every grunt out of your four-pump symphony. So how in the *fuck* do you expect me to be able to sit here and pretend like you're going to be impartial about trusting each other unless we're rehearsing with your dick in my mouth!"

I stand there, utterly aghast and truly at a loss for words, and want to disappear, to grab the first plane ticket to as far from here as I can get and never return. But all I can do is remain frozen, with my mouth hanging open like a fish.

"What? You got nothing else to say? Maybe you'll have a better time explaining your little dance metaphor to Rebecca Burgess!" Alex throws a pair of middle fingers at me and the rest of the cast. "Fuck all of you. I'm out of here."

He bursts through the doors out to the stairwell.

I turn to look at the cast and crew. Bitsie's face is almost as red as mine. Elaine wears a look of disappointment, and Eden pretends to stare at her script. Nate's jaw has dropped nearly to the floor.

"I'm so sorry, everyone," I say. "I don't...I didn't mean to..."

Danny is smiling from ear to ear, like he is watching the drama unfold on a Bravo reality series. "From where I was sitting, it sounded like way more than four pumps. And I don't hear Bitsie complaining."

"Danny!" Bitsie scolds through gritted teeth.

"Sorry! But if it helps, I think you two make an adorable couple..."

"I have to go talk to Alex." I hurry toward the door to catch up with him, but my fucking OCD pulls me back. My teeth chatter non-stop while I rip open the breakroom's fridge door and slam it shut. Only then am I allowed to rush to the stairwell.

The last thing I hear before leaving is Danny calling out, "Run to him, Mike! Run to him!"

I'm up the stairs in a flash and maybe ten feet into the garden when I hear the door open behind me.

"Mike! Wait up!" Nate calls, sprinting to catch up to me.

"I know, Nate. I messed up."

"Yeah, you did. What the hell were you thinking?"

I shake my head, unable to get into the details right now. "I don't know. Bitsie and I have been rehearsing for the last couple of nights after work. She showed up unannounced to my room, when I was already upset about seeing this goddamn ghost that won't leave me alone. One thing sort of led to another."

"Slow down a second." Nate grabs me by the shoulder, but I can't let up.

"Didn't you hear what he said? He's going to go to Rebecca."

"No, he's not. Alex Keating is a pussy who needs this job more than you do. He's just bluffing to get his way. Now hold up a minute and talk to me."

I want to believe Nate, but my heart is beating a mile a minute, and breaking my stride leaves my whole body vibrating with unspent inertia. "What?"

"First off, I just need to know...Was it you or her?"

"I don't know what you mean," I say. My head is either shaking or shivering. I don't know which.

"Look...I know you're not a Weinstein asshole. But you have to tell me, and you need be honest. Who initiated?"

"*She* did. I tried to pull away. It's just been so long. I've been so lonely. It all happened too fast. I don't know what else to say other than I royally screwed up in a moment of desperation and weakness."

Nate nods. "Okay. That's good. I mean, I wish you could have ended up with literally anyone else to finally find some intimacy with. But long-term, I think this is a big step for you."

"I really can't think about that right now."

"I know, but, Mike...You need to take a step back right now. Breathe, okay? Tell me exactly what happened."

I try, but it comes out as a juddery mess. "We've been opening up to each other...in a way I haven't done since...since back then. She asked me what the play meant to me, and I don't know why, but I felt safe and I told her the story. *Our* story, about Brie. There's something about Bitsie that just makes me feel like I can say anything. When I told her, I thought she'd call me a monster. But instead, she kissed me. And now, it just feels like I'm on the edge of a cliff and it's all going to end like—"

"Listen to me." Nate grabs me by both shoulders and forces me to look him dead in the eyes. "This is nothing like last time, all right? You and Bitsie are both adults. She came to you. No one's going to get hurt here. Not like Brie. Are you hearing me?"

I wipe away a pair of tears threatening to make a prison break from my eyes. "It still all feels like my fault. I just don't know how much more of this I can take."

"Well, I do, and you're stronger than you give yourself credit for. You think I'd be here right now if I believed otherwise? I know I put you through the wringer, asking you to come back here. I know it seems like everything's falling apart. But maybe this is just what you need—a catalyst to find your way back on your feet. You've been treading water for fifteen years, and now look at you...You let someone get close enough to accept you for who you are. I mean, fuck...You told someone about Brie. That's huge!"

"You're not mad?"

"*Mad*? This is what I was hoping would happen! Again, not quite like this...But I thought maybe, if you came back home, you could finally work your way through all your shit, like I did, and come out the other side as a human instead of this robot you've become that's severed himself from humanity."

I force myself to take another deep breath. There's something in Nate's words which ring true. I may have made an incredibly inappropriate decision in *who* to come out to, but I did finally open up to someone. "You really think this could be a good thing?"

"In the long run, yeah. I think you're definitely going to have to do some groveling, and if anyone's getting their dick sucked today, it's Alex. But yeah. You told me yesterday you were being haunted. This is it. Whether this Chester guy is legit or not, the real ghost you've been dealing with this whole time is Brie. And you finally confronted it. You're figuring out how to move on. And, of course, it's going to be messy. When in our lives have things ever *not* been a total shitshow? But this is your moment, right here, man. I swear to God, you're going to look back at this week one day as the turning point in your life."

I want to believe in his unending optimism, more than anything. And maybe he *is* right. At this point, I barely even know which way is up.

"What about Alex? The play?"

"Man, fuck the play. Let Alex quit, for all I care. You realize *this right here* is why I brought you back to Seattle, right?"

A numbness trickles down from my head to my toes, and a strange sense of calm envelopes. I reach in and hug Nate for the first time since I arrived in town.

"Thanks, man. I love you."

"I love you too, dude. Now forget what I just said about letting Alex quit. We totally need him. Go put on your big boy pants and do whatever it takes to get him back."

<hr>

When I reach Greenwood Terrace, Alex has his door wide open. He's digging through his drawers, and his suitcase is sitting on his coffee table. I knock and step into the frame.

"Hey, you mind if we talk?"

"Fuck off," Alex says, without looking up.

"I wanted to apologize for how heated things got back there."

"Save it for Rebecca."

"Come on, Alex. Stop packing. Enough with the threats. Let's just sit down and talk this out like adults, huh?" I try to take a step inside, but that proves to be a mistake.

Alex rushes at me and shoves me hard. I am completely unprepared for his physical assault, and I stumble. Unlike the upper-floor apartments, which have a rail just outside the unit, the first-floor rooms simply have a pair of concrete stairs leading to the street. My foot catches on one, and I fall backward.

Time slows. I wait for my head to split open on the concrete sidewalk below. Instead, my spine crashes into something malleable and metal. It still hurts, but it's a hell of a lot better than my brains being splattered across the ground.

A hand reaches out and catches me by the shoulder.

"Hey there, boss. You okay?" A bearded, filthy face looks at me, and it takes me a few seconds to recognize him as Steve, the vagrant.

He looks up at Alex, who now stands in the doorway I was just shoved from. "Hey, buddy. What's your fuckin' problem?"

"Oh shit," Alex says. "Not you again."

Once I am on my feet, Steve strides up to Alex. "Yeah, me again."

Alex points a finger at him while retreating. "Don't you take one more step, I'm warning you." He pulls out his phone. "If you trespass onto my property, I'm calling the cops. And you better believe I'll have you arrested this time."

Steve ignores Alex and enters the apartment. "Well, I just saved a man from an attempted murder. If I hadn't been there, this guy could'a been killed. I been to jail before. I ain't afraid. Are *you*?"

Alex works up the courage to step up to him, nearly shoves Steve like he did me but stops short, likely remembering what happened last time he laid a finger on the man. "I'm warning you!" Alex shouts, pressing the numbers for 911, then hovering his finger over the call button.

Steve turns his head toward me. "Your call, boss. What do you want?" Steve reaches into his pocket.

I hope to God he isn't grabbing the army-emblazoned knife he showed me the other day.

"It's fine, really. Thank you for breaking my fall. I appreciate it. But Alex and I just had a little disagreement and were about to talk it out like civilized men. Weren't we?"

Fear creeps into Alex's eyes. He glances between me and Steve and nods.

"Yeah. I guess so."

"Alex is going to put away his phone, and we're all going to go back to our day. Is that all right, Steve?"

For a minute, Steve doesn't move. Finally, he gives one nod of his head, then backs out. I reach into my pocket for my wallet, pull out a twenty, and give it to him. "Thanks again for saving me."

"Like I said, I got your back."

With Steve on his way, I slowly re-enter Alex's apartment.

"Now, are you ready to talk, or do I need to call back my muscle?" I put on a slight smile, one I hope he takes as a joke.

Alex huffs, then grabs a seat on his couch. "Fine. Let's talk."

"Thank you." I grab the desk chair, which he keeps pressed against his window, and sit opposite him. "Listen, I truly am sorry for what I said back there. I think we can both agree that things haven't really gone the way we hoped they would and it's made this process a lot harder than it should. Still, it was way out of line for me to bring your family into this, and for that, I'm sorry."

Alex bobs his head, almost imperceptibly.

"And while you are right that Bitsie and I *did* spend a night together last night, I need you to believe me that it had nothing to do with the play or how I've been regarding either of your performances."

This time, he snorts in contempt.

"You can believe me or not, but here's the bottom line. Despite the troubles you've had with me and Bitsie, I know you want to be in this play. I can see it in an actor's eyes the second it clicks for them. For you, we weren't even ten minutes into the first table read when it happened. You're not here for a paycheck or an audience. You're doing *Wherever You Go* because you're an artist and there's something about this play that means something to you. Am I right?"

Alex still won't talk, but at least now he is meeting my eyes.

"I know it was a blow losing Cassandra. The chemistry you had was undeniable. You made great dance partners. But the two of you were doing the tango, and Bitsie only knows how to do the waltz. I'll admit, it's a stupid metaphor, but do you know what I mean?"

With a grudging sigh, Alex finally speaks. "Yeah, I get it."

"Her energy is different. She changes the show simply by being in it. And I hate that it's happened this way. But my job is to put on the best production possible. The truth is, with the people we have now, this is *better* as a waltz. And I'm not saying she needs to lead the whole dance. But I need you to have enough of a working relationship that it feels like you're at least on the same stage."

Alex darts his eyes back to the floor. Tension rises in the room. His breaths grow heavy. "What if I don't know *how* to waltz?"

There it is.

The breakthrough I've been waiting for this whole time.

This is something I can work with. I give him a reassuring laugh.

"You're Alex Fucking Keating. You can learn any dance you put your mind to."

Alex and I decide we are going to take the rest of the day for him to cool off and re-read the script. He will come in fresh tomorrow with the scenes he feels he truly needs to lead and which scenes he can re-work.

I walk back to the rehearsal space, doing my best to focus on the positives. Nate said this is the breakthrough I needed, and I feel like he has never been more correct. My need to click my teeth while I walk has receded, and when I was in Alex's apartment, I didn't even think about checking his fridge or stove. Maybe this is what progress looks like.

However, the second I cross the threshold into the basement, I have five sets of eyes which bring me back to earth with a mixture of embarrassment, disappointment, and expectation.

I don't know who to address first or how to approach it, so I just start talking and hope my head catches up.

"Hey, everyone. I know that all seemed, well, bad, and I'd like to start by addressing the state of the show. I spoke to Alex at his apartment. We actually managed to have a much more calm and civilized conversation once it was just the two of us. He's not leaving, he's not reporting anyone, and in fact, he said he's going to make his best effort to be more of a team player moving forward.

"Like all of us here, Alex cares deeply about *Wherever You Go*, and even though we have very limited time to right this ship, he's determined to put in the extra effort to get everything back on track. We will be ending rehearsal early today for him to collect his thoughts and review the material, but he has invited Danny, Elaine, and Bitsie out to dinner tonight at Shakespeare's Head to work things out. He even says it's his treat, so I hope you'll all go into this with good faith.

"As for my behavior, I want to apologize, first and foremost, for the unprofessional way I carried myself in our disagreement. Not only should I have behaved in a manner more fitting as your director, but I shouldn't have let our problem spill out into the common area like this. The issues between me and Alex should have stayed private, and I'm sorry for any distress or resentment I might have created by having such a public blowout."

My eyes drift across the group. Nate is sending me vibes of support, which I need when I notice the frustration and exhaustion in Eden, the skeptical brow of Elaine, the hungry eyes of Danny, and Bitsie's clear embarrassment.

"Now, I suppose I should probably address the other elephant in the room. I guess the cat's out of the bag that Bitsie and I had...relations last night."

A heat builds between Bitsie and me, but not the kind we shared yesterday. Thankfully, Danny cuts me off before I can get any further.

"Hey, Mike...I can actually spare you an embarrassing talk. While you were gone, Bitsie already spilled all the tea."

My eyes widen. The first thing which enters my head is the story I shared about Brie. As if reading my mind, Nate cocks an eyebrow and gives a quick shake of the head, indicating that she left out that part of the story.

Danny continues. "This may be controversial or whatever, but I'm just gonna throw it out there. I think you two are cute together. She made it super clear that this has nothing to do with the play. There's no ick factor. I think I can speak for everyone here when I ask, who *hasn't* had a torrid romance during a show? That's half the fun of this job!"

Elaine furrows her brow, looking more offended by his words than mine.

Danny continues. "As long as you two keep it profesh in the office, I don't care what you do on your own time. In fact, I wish *I* was getting some right now."

"I would never let any sort of personal relationship compromise the show. That's the last thing I want," I say.

Elaine shrugs. "I've seen worse, though I wouldn't put it as emphatically as Danny. Just don't keep me up at night, okay?"

I nod. "Understood. Well, with all of that taken care of, I guess all that's left to say is...enjoy the rest of your day."

Danny, Elaine, Bitsie, and Nate all take off. Eden remains in her seat, clearly waiting to have words with me.

"Eden?" I pull up a seat next to her. "How are you doing?"

"Mike, I'm a professional. I've seen everything. That said, I expected more from you, in both the way you handled Alex and your highly inappropriate relationship with Bitsie. I hope you meant what you said and this doesn't interfere with the rest of rehearsals because I don't think I need to remind you that we're way behind schedule."

"I know. I'm sorry."

"You didn't do anything illegal, but contrary to Danny's sentiments, I definitely think what you're doing is gross. But I'm your stage manager, and my number one job is to make sure this thing is ready to open on time. And on that note, we're supposed to start tech on Monday, and we are not going to be ready for that. As much as I hate to say it, I think it's best if we talk to Rebecca about pushing it back a few days and potentially scaling back from four preview nights to two."

I nod. "I think that's a good idea. Thank you."

"Don't thank me, Mike. I'm just doing my job."

All things considered, the meeting went better than I ever could have imagined. I pack up my things, then get ready to go revisit the script for this new and improved Alex Keating. This time, when I exit the rehearsal hall, I make the conscious choice not to touch the refrigerator while I head toward the door.

To my pleasant surprise, my superstitious worries about the fridge are left behind in the basement. I swear I almost feel lighter while I skip up the stairs. As soon as I reach the top level of the winding stairwell, I find Bitsie waiting for me in the museum's garden.

"Hey, Mike...Can we talk?"

"Yeah, that's probably a good idea. I'm really sorry about everything."

She scrunches her small, bony shoulders up to her ears and gives me a faint smile. "Yeah. That was awkward."

"I think it's probably for the best if we sort of cool it, for everyone's sake."

Bitsie nods. Even though we are talking about backing off, we are standing so close that I sense heat radiating off her skin. It makes me want nothing more than to wrap my arms around her and carry her back inside the now-vacated rehearsal space.

"This may sound crazy, but what if we didn't?" she says.

"Didn't what?"

"Cool it. I mean, obviously, let's give everyone a day or two, but I really feel like there's a connection here. I don't want it to end."

Something in my long-cemented heart cracks. Not just blood, but the very essence of life pumps back into my body. "I feel the same way."

"Okay...So let's table things for tonight, maybe tomorrow. But after..." She allows the words to linger.

"Yeah, after."

Her cheeks turn a slight shade of pink.

"I know this isn't the right time, but what are you planning on doing after the show opens?"

I shake my head. "I have an offer to do *Caucasian Chalk Circle* in Austin about a week after opening, but I haven't committed yet."

"Do you think, maybe, you could stay a while? With me?"

My stone heart crumbles, and I begin to picture my time with her as something potentially more than just a momentary breakthrough. I imagine myself putting down roots, even briefly entertaining the idea of having a place to call home, which isn't just a video of my therapist's office.

"I would love that."

She grabs me by the lapel of my coat, climbs onto her tippy-toes, and kisses me on the cheek.

In that instant, the heat overtakes me, and my mind is pulled into another vision.

My muscles moving...The pressure it takes to shove her back inside and over the guardrail...Leaning forward and watching her head and limbs pinball off the railings all the way down four flights...Her body landing with a splattering crunch on the concrete below...

As soon as she pulls her lips away from my cheek, I am right back where we are. It takes everything I have to not display the horror I have just witnessed in my head.

"I'll see you later," she says, thankfully not noticing whatever wires just shorted out in my brain.

After she leaves, I pause for a minute to collect myself. With everyone else going out tonight, I text Nate to see if he wants to grab dinner.

> Sorry, bud. I got a date. You're on your own tonight.

It's only one thirty in the afternoon, but by the time I reach Greenwood Terrace, the sun is creeping behind the buildings across the street. I check my phone and am frustrated and frightened to see it's nearly five. Furthermore, my bag is heavier than it should be.

I open it up and discover a bottle of wine, along with a sandwich from the deli I have no memory of buying. Though I want to scream, the proximity of my cast makes me feel like I need to cage my own fear. If they hear me lose it now, I don't think I could ever recover my already crumbling image in their eyes.

My throat is dry. I try to swallow, but my mouth is a desert. As horrible as the visions and interactions with Chester are, these bouts of lost time are perhaps the most disturbing thing of all. I have no memory of what I have done during these periods. So much of my life revolves around me taking comfort in routine and the power which comes with controlling myself and my environment, but I am completely helpless and not in command of my body.

Despite what we talked about, maybe it is for the best if Bitsie and I maintain some personal distance for a while. So far, she trusts me, finds me flawed but otherwise decent. How much strain, how much trauma, would I dump on her if I told her everything that is really going on with me? Jesus, what if she were to see my spontaneous writing sessions? She would probably have me in handcuffs and off to a psychiatric ward.

I climb the stairs to my apartment just as Alex and the rest leave theirs to head off to dinner. Before I mount the last flight, I close my eyes and take a deep breath, bracing myself in case Chester is waiting for me outside my room. My hand begins to itch where I got the spider bite, and I scratch at it until the tickle becomes a burn. When I am ready, I open my eyes and climb.

To my pleasant surprise, the space is empty.

Of course, that relief is only short-lived.

As soon as I enter my apartment, the smell of cigarette smoke curls up my nose. I search the room for Chester but find the room vacant. There is that heavy feeling, like when I was in the rehearsal bathroom. An oppressive force bears down on me and puts all my senses on high alert, like I'm being watched from the shadows.

I try to force it out of my head, try to ignore it by pulling out the sandwich and wine. After grabbing a corkscrew from my kitchenette, I drink straight from the bottle while sitting on my couch. I'm convinced alcohol has become my only defense to protect myself against Chester's visits. Or maybe it just makes me feel less overwhelmed when he does show up.

Even through the smell of smoke, a competing scent lingers, one which reminds me of Bitsie.

Although I have no memory of ordering it, the sandwich is just how I like it: plain turkey and cheese, with a packet of mustard on the side. I take a bite and nearly choke.

The sandwich comes alive in my mouth, filled with prickling, squirming sensations accompanied by bitter flavors. Something hard crunches in my molars, then explodes a sickening, acrid juice into my mouth. I spit it out, finding a mushed-up ball of half-masticated legs, shells, and entrails of bugs.

When I drop the sandwich, dozens of tiny legs skitter across it. A half-eaten spider spits green goo from its abdomen, and a centipede flails wildly without a head. Cockroaches, beetles, maggots, and worms squirm and crawl out from the bread and across my fingers. I flick my hand away, sending the bugs flying, and fight the overwhelming urge to retch. Then I grab for the wine and chug until the taste of the putrid critters are overwhelmed by the strong red drink.

"Oh dear...It seems someone has mishandled your order." Chester's voice leads his body. He steps out from the shadow of my closet.

"Fuck off!" I shout. "I've had enough of this."

"You sound stressed, Mike. Why don't you sit down for another writing session?"

"I'm not doing those anymore. I'm *done* with you."

He shakes his head. "But I'm not done with you, Mike. Not until you kill Beth.

"I'm not killing anyone. No matter how many times you burn me with your cigarettes or make me eat bugs. It's not real. *None* of it is." I reach down and grab the top bread of the sandwich, peeling it back to reveal nothing more than turkey and cheese. "You can torture me all you want, but I know your game now. It's all just projection. Parlor tricks. You can't actually do anything. I'm sorry that someone killed you and your family, I am. But if I've learned anything since coming back here, it's that you can't just dwell on the past. You have to find a way to move on."

Chester snickers. "Easy for you to say. You're not trapped here."

"I was. For years. I know you've been watching me. I'm sure you've heard me talking to my therapist, to Nate." I point toward the room next to me, where he and his family were killed, two units over from where Brie died. "I've been trapped in this building, just like you have, for the last fifteen years. There's only one way out, and that's *through*."

Chester lets out a trio of *tsks*, shaking his head. "You can preach all you want, Mikey boy...Pretend like you're not just as hopeless as I am... We both know you've been dealing with ghosts long before you met me. And you're still missing the big picture."

"And what is that?" I demand.

"I'm not the ghost you came to confront."

"No shit. But I already told Bitsie everything about Brie–"

"Stop calling her that!" he roars, his voice transforming into something inhuman and monstrous. "Her name is Beth. You *will* enact my revenge, and you *will* see the truth before this is all over. You can fight me all you want, but sooner or later, you'll realize I'm here to help you."

I let out a cynical laugh. "How is *any* of this helping me? You want me to become a killer!"

"You've already done it before. What's one more time?"

"It wasn't my fault." The words burst out of me for the first time ever.

There hasn't been a day that has gone by that I haven't lived with the firm belief that what happened to Brie rested entirely on my shoulders. But I'm through being haunted. By Brie *and* by this asshole. I am done with all of it.

"It wasn't. My. Fault!" I repeat the words, each one spitting from my mouth like a bullet directed at the specter before me.

Chester stands there, unimpressed. In fact, a smile slowly creeps across his face. "It saddens me to see you in such denial. I really do think we should sit down for another writing session."

"I already told you...I'm not doing another one of those. Not now, not—"

A lightning bolt of pain strikes my skull, and I am seated at my desk, with my laptop in front of me. Chester looms over my shoulder, his hands gripped tightly over my wrists. The harder I try to fight him, the stronger he gets.

He pushes my hands onto the keyboard and forces me to type.

Spontaneous Writing: Session 10

I love my family more than anything, but directing was so much easier when it was just me and Susie. While it wasn't ideal for me to leave for months at a time, she understood my art, respected it.

My whole world changed when she told me she got pregnant with our son, Caleb. I'd directed dozens of plays, produced art all over the world. But now, I had created it. From our love, we made something truly amazing, someone that transcended all work that had preceded him.

He was my boy. My everything. And I failed him.

I thought it would be an adventure to bring them with me on a trip to America. To let Caleb see more of the world. And, of course, I thought it would be a chance to spend more time with him. Instead, I uprooted him from his school, his friends, his home, to a dingy little apartment in a town where he knew no one.

To make matters worse, Susie had become ill

with a virus that kept her bedridden for almost
the entire duration of our stay. She was tired
all the time, and instead of visits to the Space
Needle, museums, and the Point Defiance Zoo and
Aquarium, Caleb just lingered in a room, dying of
boredom while I worked. That was, until he met
Beth.

She was a girl nearly his age, dark hair,
bright eyes. Sound familiar, Mike? She lived
nearby, and like Caleb, had no friends, and
woefully absent parents. The two grew close
rather quickly. At first, I was elated that he'd
found a friend. But as the days turned into
weeks, I began to notice changes in the way Caleb
behaved; crass words that he'd learned from Beth.
Things that were outright disturbing. They'd
taken to playing under a bridge and taunted the
poor tramps that lingered. They stole wine, and
on several occasions, I came home to a drunken
eleven-year-old.

One day, I even found our boy with a switchblade in his pocket. I made him swear to never
see her again. I didn't know what else to do. He
raged, threatened me and Susie that we would be
sorry if we forbade them from seeing each other.
It became so serious I considered pulling out of
the show, collecting my family, and returning
home to London.

Then the day came, when I returned from work
late. At first I thought my eyes were deceiving
me. Caleb was standing over our bed holding a
knife. Susie was already dead, her throat carved
open by my own son's hands. Beth stood behind
him, laughing as if this were some game.

I ran to my boy, my once beautiful innocent
boy, corrupted by that horrible girl. I pried the

knife from his hand. He fought me, bit at me as I tried to carry him out. I can still feel my wife's blood all over him as he raged against me.

Then I felt the blade. Beth had a knife of her own, which she used to slice behind my kneecaps. My legs gave out on me, I fell to the floor.

Caleb wriggled free, and the two of them took turns stabbing me in the stomach. As I bled out, I watched her turn to my son. I'll never forget her words.

"Now it's your turn."

Even after everything he'd done, my heart broke as I saw the shock in his eyes as she betrayed him and stabbed him in the throat. He toppled over. And the last thing I ever saw was her on top of him, stabbing him over, and over, and over again.

CHAPTER 10

I am not just typing. It is as if I am living Chester's last day while he forces me to write. My trance is broken when a bloodcurdling scream comes from somewhere in the building.

The horrific sound breaks whatever spell Chester cast on me. I surge to my feet, no longer feeling his presence. Sunlight pours through the window. Somehow, it's already morning.

I run outside to find Danny and Elaine standing on the sidewalk, staring in horror through the window of Alex's apartment.

Acid boils in my stomach when I peer inside. There is another tear across the mesh of the window, and Alex Keating is splayed out across his bed in an acutely familiar position. His throat is cut. Blood paints the walls, even the ceiling.

"Oh God," I mutter, pulling out my phone and calling 911.

I feel sick, weak at the knees, but I can't stop staring at him for however many minutes pass until the paramedics and police arrive. Every detail of the gory scene is almost identical to how I remember Chester's wife.

It is like my head is made of molasses, but slowly, eventually, one terrifying thought seeps through.

Did I do this?

I fought against Chester, almost goaded him last night before he had me sit down and write about his own death. But there is no way that took nine hours. What the hell else did he have me do while he was at the wheel?

Panic streaks through me when lights and sirens come blaring up from around the corner. The police break down the door, which was still locked, to get inside and secure the crime scene.

Dully, somewhere in the distance, Danny and Elaine moan and scream that they had just been with him last night, that everything was finally getting better.

Eventually, the police sit each of us down separately to take statements. I explain that I was in my apartment all last night, which, as far as I know, is the truth. But the whole time I am explaining my whereabouts and total lack of alibi, I am interrogating myself as much as they are questioning me. They ask if I know of any grudges he could have had.

That is when the molasses drips further and another horrifying thought enters my head. But it is so disgusting I cannot even bring myself to say it out loud. I'm nearly sick just thinking about it.

If, somehow, Bitsie *was* Beth, she would know how to position him, how to kill him in just the same way that Chester's wife was murdered.

The police ask again, "Is there anyone else you can think of who might have had a grudge against Alex Keating?"

I hate myself for saying it, but out of some sick sense of self preservation, I do it anyway—I describe the multiple altercations Steve the vagrant had with Alex, how he described his military service and showed me his knife, how I had suspected he had it in his pocket yesterday when he pushed his way into Alex's apartment.

What's even worse, while I am telling the story, I'm trying to find a way to fit what feels like a square peg into a round hole. Steve told me he had my back.

I don't know for sure that he wasn't the one to break into the apartment and rob Alex the first time. No one does. But he *did* have the evidence on him. He was wearing Alex's clothes. Who's to say Steve didn't break back into the apartment last night, the same way as before, to eliminate a perceived threat? Worse even than that, what if he did it in a deranged plot to protect me?

Jesus...that is almost as bad as the other two scenarios racing through my head. If any of the three of us did this, I can't help but feel like it is still all on me. My world is spiraling out of control, and I find myself once again clicking my teeth, well past the point where my jaw tightens and aches.

One, one, five, four, three, two, one. One, one, five, four, three, two, four, two, one.

The day crawls by. My insides squirm with each second that passes. I relive every moment of the last week and try to find something to explain this. There was no reason that I would have had to kill Alex, other than Chester using me to prove some sort of point.

I remember the words I so callously threw at Chester, believing the time to be a moment of breakthrough for me. *It wasn't my fault.* In my attempt to assert my own personal growth against Chester, could he have made me do this to force my reevaluation of that statement? To make me realize I am very much capable of killing someone? If so, why not just have me go kill Beth directly?

Hours tick slowly away while I dreamwalk my way through phone call after phone call. A conversation with Eden...She talks about canceling the show, asks me what I want to do. I don't have an answer. Nate is next, offering condolences and remarks of incredulity.

I don't snap out of my stupor until a knock sounds at my door. It's Bitsie, red-eyed and tearful. She throws her arms around me, sobbing. And just like that, my brain is on fire, the molasses melts away, and I finally break down in tears with her. We hold each other on the couch while she tells me of the wonderful evening they had, how Alex apologized to her, how he seemed like a changed man from the stuck-up nightmare we'd had to endure before. How excited she was to show me they were going to finally get this play back on track...

I feel her warmth against me, her hot tears mixing with mine, and truly believe there is no way she could have done this. It's insane.

No, Mike. You're insane.

If it wasn't her, it must have been me.

I want to push her away, tell her that I am sick, dangerous. That I will hurt her if she stays. But the closer she curls herself into me, the harder it is to pull back. The next thing I know, we are back in my bed.

Some mixture of grief, loss, and an intense burning for life has led me back inside her. We are made of nothing but pure, raw emotion. Of hurt, love, fear, and fragility, all wrapped up in the clawing, primal grasp of knowing we only have this moment. Any second, everything could be ripped away from us.

There is no such thing as control. Just chaos.

Monday morning rolls around after a night of exhausted, dreamless sleep. A dark day, both for the theater world at large and The Burgess. There are no visits from Chester. Just me and Bitsie, holding each other. I shut off my alarm and turn on airplane mode to silence the never-ending procession of calls I don't want to answer.

Eventually, we pull ourselves up, and I check my phone, seeing over a dozen voicemails.

I have missed my Monday appointment with Dr. Jules. As strange as it is, after everything that has happened since last Friday, I don't know that there is anything she can do for me anymore. If I explain to her that I am being haunted by a ghost, she will think I have lost my mind. And if I explain that I had a breakthrough with Bitsie, I worry she would try and talk me down, to walk back the progress I know I have made.

Also, there is no way I can show her my latest writing sessions. She would have me committed.

Nate has called several times. So has Eden. I will talk to them later.

Finally, there are three missed calls from a number my smartphone suggests is Seattle Police. I call them back first. If there is any evidence of me in the apartment, I would rather they arrest me now and spare me from having to talk to anyone else.

"Mr. O'Brien?" a man's voice says. He identifies himself as Officer Coffer.

I remember the name as the cop who interviewed me yesterday.

"Yes?"

"I just wanted to inform you that we have a suspect in custody. We found the man you described, one Steve Drake, wandering the streets late yesterday afternoon. He was heavily intoxicated and on several drugs. He had a few bloodstains on his clothes. We're running labs now to try and match them with Mr. Keating. We still haven't found the weapon, but at this time, we believe him to be the man who committed the murder in your building."

I let out a heavy sigh, failing to feel the sense of relief I had hoped to have upon learning of my potential innocence. "Thank you, Officer."

"We'll call you if we have any more details." The officer hangs up.

"What is it?" Bitsie asks, rubbing my back with her warm, comforting hand.

"They found Steve. They think it was him."

"No." Bitsie's hands slap against her mouth. She seems just as horrified to hear it was Steve.

"I remember you said you knew him."

She nods. "I volunteer at the homeless shelter when I have time, but I owe Steve my life. He and I have known each other for years. I just can't believe..." Her words turn into a hiccup of sobs, and she starts to cry again.

This time, it is my turn to comfort her.

She is an actress, but there is no way this could be a performance. Yet even having heard about the evidence, something inside of me still feels like I am not getting the whole story. I just don't know if it's from her or me.

My attention swings sharply when my phone comes to life in my hands. Eden is reaching out again. Our call is short; she wants me to come to the office above the theater to speak to her and Rebecca Burgess about the state of the show. I dial Nate, in case she hasn't already reached him, and he agrees to meet with the rest of us in thirty minutes.

As much as I want to stay in bed with Bitsie, to just hide under the covers for a week or a month, I pull myself together. After everything that has happened, I still believe in Nate's script, in all the work we have put in. But if I am going to be able to convince Rebecca Burgess and Eden to continue, I need to look like I am in my right mind.

Nate and I arrive outside the building at the same time and head up the stairs. Rebecca's office is small, like every other space not directly dedicated to the presentation of the theater for ticket holders. Though the productions here have won countless awards over the years, Rebecca keeps a humble office, free of accolades. Like any good theater owner, she lives for art, not awards.

Rebecca sits in her chair opposite Eden, who is already seated, a heavily revised schedule in front of her. The paper is almost impossible to read, with all the scratches, re-writes, and lines ending in arrows. There is only one other chair in the office. Nate gestures for me to sit in it while he stands behind us.

"Mike, I wish we could be meeting under better circumstances this morning," Rebecca says. "Lord knows this theater has had its share of tragedies, but I can't recall a time when a show has lost both of its leads in such a horrific manner. How are you holding up?"

This is where I put my acting face on. "I'm hanging in there. I have honestly no words for how horrible this truly is. Alex Keating was a tremendous talent and a wonderful human being."

I can feel a side-eye coming from Eden, but she is not the one I need to convince right now.

"Just awful." Rebecca adjusts her glasses and runs a hand through her raven-black hair. "I hate that we even need to have this meeting, that this conversation needs to take place, but we have to address the business side of things. We're meeting here today to talk about whether or not, as they say, the show must go on."

I give her a slow and sympathetic nod and let the room breathe before I answer. "Personally, I think *Wherever You Are* should continue. I know we would need to talk to the actors, to see if they are still up to continue, but I truly believe that Alex had his heart in this show and he would want us to keep going in his memory."

Rebecca Burgess nods. "I know we've already had our fair share of setbacks. Tech should have started last week and was postponed to tomorrow, cutting preview nights down from four to two. If we replaced our lead now, would it even be possible to open this Friday?"

"I believe so. Danny and Bitsie already have great chemistry. They've known each other from previous productions and are very close. If we re-cast him as Husband, I know they would be willing to work after-hours to get up to speed. The show already is extremely sparse in terms of lighting, sound, and set changes. We just have the four set pieces, and aside from the storm scene, our lighting cues are pretty simple.

"Today's Monday. I think if we picked back up tomorrow with run-throughs, we could rally the troops to squeeze all of tech down to just Wednesday, do dress rehearsals Thursday, and then open Friday as planned. This would mean zero previews, and it's obviously going to need to be refined over the course of the run, but I truly believe it's possible to at least have something presentable.

Rebecca looks over to Eden. "Your thoughts?"

"If this were any other show, under any other circumstances, I'd say this would be impossible. That being said, Danny was already Husband's understudy. He knows the lines, and he wants to be here. I'm not worried about him or Bitsie. But if we commit to this, we need to pull off two small miracles. The first would be that everything from here on out goes as smoothly as possible, which, given the course of events so far, we all know is asking a lot. Tech was already pushed from three comfortable days down to a tight two. Given the low amount of cues in this show, I think it's possible to pull some overtime and crunch it down to a marathon of a single day.

"The second issue is that if we move Danny up to the Husband role, then we need to recast Danny's role. Even with the pool of actors we have on our shortlist, we would have to put up a casting call today, which would only give–"

"I could do it," I jump in.

Both women stare at me as if I just suggested using Alex's corpse to play the role.

"Are you sure about that, Mike?" Rebecca asks. "You're already stretched so thin."

"I did some acting back in college. I'm sure I can handle it. The parts are small. Obviously, I already know them. I can do this."

"Mike," Rebecca says, her voice dripping with concern. "I know you feel a deep connection and a sense of obligation to this show, but as you know, directors don't typically even stay in town after opening night, never mind stay through the entire run. Also, there's the fact that you can't be in two places at once. We need you next to Eden during tech, not standing on the stage."

I think about Bitsie, how she asked me to stay in town. Now I have a real excuse.

"There's other people in the crew my height. We can get literally anyone to fill my role for tech. I want to do this. I need to."

Eden looks like she wants to protest but bites her tongue. Rebecca narrows her eyes and studies me.

"Well, if you're sure..."

"I am."

"All right. If you can get the cast to sign on to the new schedule, we'll cancel previews and open Friday night."

"Thank you. You won't regret it," I say, trying to convince myself as much as everyone else in the room.

The meeting with the cast goes surprisingly well. As I suspected, Danny is totally onboard to take on the role of the Husband. He and Bitsie agree that, rather than sit and dwell on the sadness of Alex's loss, they want to jump straight into it, not even wasting the rest of the day. We head down to the rehearsal space and start a run-through ASAP.

Elaine isn't exactly hard to convince, but I wouldn't call her enthused either. She asks to remain at home for the rest of her day off, to mourn, which is completely understandable.

As much as I hate to admit it, we are no more than twenty minutes into our first rehearsal with our new Husband and Wife when Bitsie and Danny find a rhythm that I can't deny is miles beyond anything I have seen in the past few weeks. Though the last thing Alex ever said to me was that he was ready to rededicate himself to being a team player, Danny is practically falling over himself to follow Bitsie's lead. It feels so natural, watching them work together.

To be totally honest, I wasn't sure how well Danny would fit in playing a straight romantic lead. In my experience, around sixty percent of the male actors I work with are gay, and maybe fifteen percent of those actors can really sell the role of a straight romantic lead. As bombastic as Danny is in real life, he is a true professional and plays the role of Husband with a complexity and emotional range Alex never quite seemed to hit, even with Cassandra.

He is loud and obnoxious in the argument scenes but never as over-the-top as Alex was. And in the quiet, intimate scenes, where the audience is reminded that these two are meant to truly be in love—separated by their own traumas and the cyclical nature of their inability to move past their pain—he is a revelation. The way he holds her, caresses her face, kisses her, is gentle and loving enough that I am lost in their characters. So much so that, once or twice, I forget where I am and almost feel a twinge of jealousy.

It makes me think about my own budding relationship with Bitsie, how strong my feelings are for her despite how quickly things have moved. After her reaction this morning to learning about Steve's likely involvement in the murder, I have decided I am going to make a point of breaking my normal cycle of constant rumination and doom spiraling. I'm going to follow my heart for once and trust her.

Eden has a metric ton of behind-the-scenes work to take care of for the rest of the day, so it is just Nate and me overseeing the rehearsal in the basement. Even he leans over and whispers that this is going better than he ever imagined. Maybe there is a chance we can pull this thing off after all.

While I am focused on their performances for today, I remain in my seat and simply read out the lines for Elaine and myself. We can work on integrating the two of us into the show tomorrow. Right now, we need to focus on what is most important.

***

Tuesday morning comes too fast, and my blood is replaced with anxiety. What the hell was I thinking, volunteering to act in a professional play on top of my directorial duties, dealing with the compounding catastrophes which have befallen us as a group, and, of course, my own demons haunting my head and home?

For all my fears, the one relief is that Bitsie and Danny are giving an even better performance today, so much so that it feels like they have been at this together since the beginning. The only instances where things take a turn for the worse are whenever it's my cue to step in. For the sake of time and security, I hold my script while I attempt to act, glancing occasionally at lines to a play I believed I had memorized in its entirety by now.

By the end of the day, everyone seems to be in higher spirits than I expected. I give notes to Bitsie and Danny. While they review them, Nate pulls me aside to give me some notes of his own.

"So, how'd I do?" I ask.

"Of all the Brother/Doctor/Neighbor performances I've ever seen, this one is by far the most recent."

I give him a smirk. "Come on. I'm not *that* bad, am I?"

"We just need to get you more comfortable in the roles. When's the last time you actually acted?"

"I played The Wizard in *Wizard of Oz* in college. It was the only role that didn't require singing," I admit.

Nate pats me on the shoulder. "So you're a bit rusty. Honestly, you're not the worst I've seen come through here. One guy vomited on stage during the first preview of *Twelfth Night*, and he was only playing Fabian. As long as you keep all your bodily fluids inside, you'll probably have one up on him."

"Thanks for the vote of confidence," I say, with just a hint of sarcasm.

"Tell you what, Bitsie and Danny are going to be rehearsing together tonight. How about I come over and run lines with you? Give you a taste of your own medicine and let someone else boss you around for once." He smirks. "We'll grab some sushi to-go, then turn you into the best side character The Burgess Theater has ever seen."

Two floors below me, Bitsie and Danny are hard at work while I wait for Nate to arrive. I made a point of taking all the remaining booze in my fridge, stuffing it into my trash can, and covering it with some crumpled-up paper towels to hide the evidence. As much as I have been honest with him about ghosts, Bitsie, and dealing with Brie's death, I'm still not ready to tell him about my lack of sobriety.

Part of me is trying to convince myself that, if he knows I am drinking, it may weaken his resolve and put him on a slippery slope. But there is an honesty bug crawling through my head, insisting that I'm just too ashamed to tell him the truth.

He knocks on my door, the same way he has for as long as I have known him. Seven knocks to the sting of "Shave and a Haircut." True to his word, he comes with tidings of sushi.

We're about halfway through a plate of rainbow rolls when he asks me, out of the blue, "So, Mike, how are you really doing? And no bullshit."

"No bullshit?" I say, accompanied by a heavy breath. "I don't even know. This whole thing has been such a rollercoaster, in ways I never could have imagined. I appreciate why you really brought me here; dealing with Brie's death is something that I'd never even started to move past. You forced me to confront it, and though I didn't think I'd be able to, somehow, you knew I'd be able to at least start to see a light at the end of the tunnel. Just like when we were young, you know me better than I do."

"What can I say, it's a gift. That's why I'm the writer." Nate points a pair of chopsticks at himself between bites.

"And then there's Bitsie. I don't even know where to start with her. She's brought something out from inside of me that I didn't even know still existed. She's all I can think about, aside from the play' and *you know who*. Is that wrong?"

"Nah, man. You're infatuated. It's kind of cool. Even in the old days, you never really had a girlfriend or anything. I think she could be good for you, so long as you stop writing weird shit about murdering her in your journal."

I fling an empty hand at my laptop, casting it off with a gesture. "I'm done with that shit. No more spontaneous writing. In fact, I missed an appointment with my therapist today for the first time in almost five years, and I'm not even worried about it. I'm even considering telling her that we should take a break for a while."

"Well, shit. Good for you, man. I mean, not for the non-refundable deposit I'm sure you've eaten for the session. Also, you probably should talk to a professional about discovering a dead co-worker in your building. But, you know, aside from that, it's about time you started confiding in real people that you don't have to pay."

"I think there's probably a lot of stuff with Alex that I'll need to unpack at some point. Right now, though, I think I just need to keep my head down and focus on what's here in front of me."

"Whatever you need to get through it. As long as it works, it can't be bad, right?"

We finish our meals. Nate collects the paper plates and heads over to the trash, and I am halfway to my bed to grab my script before a chill runs through me. I smell smoke. That acrid, cancerous cloud from a cigarette freezes my legs in place.

Chester.

"You all right?" Nate asks, catching me frozen while I stare at the man in my closet.

My one comfort is that, of anyone to be with me when I see the ghost, it is Nate.

"He's here."

"Oh shit, the ghost?" Nate says with just a little too much excitement. "What's he doing?"

The cherry of the cigarette in the darkest recess of my room casts a dim glow on Chester's face. "He's just standing in my closet, staring at me."

Nate shakes out his arms and neck. "Oh man, you're giving me the heebie-jeebies."

Chester's mouth curls up into a wicked grin. He has something horrible planned for me. Chester steps forward, and I brace for the pain of whatever psychic torture he is about to inflict.

"Oh fuck! What the fuck!" Nate screams, stumbling backward.

"You can see him?" I ask.

"Holy shit! What the hell, man!" Nate trips over the trash can while Chester strides up to me.

Chester pulls the cigarette from his mouth and presses it into the coat of his jacket. The thing ignites like it's soaked in kerosene. His whole body immolates. His hair is a torch. His skin blisters, chars, and eventually melts from his face while he laughs maniacally, so loud it drowns out Nate's screams.

"Enough!" I shout, bringing my foot up to kick his burning body away from me.

My foot passes straight through him. As if he were made of flash paper, the flames snap him up in an instant.

"He's actually real!" Nate hollers.

While I know I should be afraid, validation pours through my veins. I'm not the only one. This means I'm not crazy. Chester is real. *Ghosts* are real. "I can't believe this! You saw him!"

"This is the ghost that's been haunting you this whole time? With all this fire and shit?"

"Yeah," I say. "Well, sometimes, it's bugs. This was the first time he's been on fire. He put out a cigarette on my hand once."

"Jesus Christ. No wonder you've been worrying about losing it. If I saw that guy coming after me every day, I'd be in the psychiatric ward."

My relief is short-lived. Up until now, Chester has never done anything just for shock value. Every move he has made has been part of an attempt to get me to kill Beth.

The moment I realize why he finally came out from the shadows is the exact minute Nate's expression changes.

"What the hell is this?" He is sitting on the floor, and scattered around him are the hidden bottles of beer and wine which tumbled out of the trash can he knocked over. "Mike, have you been drinking?"

A cocktail of horror and rage mixes inside of me. I hate Chester almost as much as I despise myself at this moment. And I don't even know how to start explaining.

"I, well..."

"After you accused me of not holding onto *my* sobriety, you were drinking this whole time?"

"It's not like that. The first time, it was an accident. I thought I was drinking a sparkling water. And then Chester tricked me the second time into thinking it was a ginger ale."

Nate picks up the trash can and dumps it out on the floor. A dozen empty beers, along with three wine bottles. A sour, stale smell wafts through the room. He looks up at me, and my excuses shrivel. I feel weak and worthless. A new kind of shame, one that is different, almost worse than the guilt of Brie, bursts its way across every nerve of my body.

Still, my mouth keeps running, trying to justify my actions. "And then, when this damned ghost started coming after me, it felt like the only way to get him to leave me alone was to have a drink."

"*Have a drink*?" Nate's words are measured, a calm before a storm. "This isn't just *a* drink, Mike. This is a lot of fucking alcohol."

"I know. I wanted to tell you. I just—"

"You were too chickenshit? What's wrong with you, man?"

I hang my head and give a limp shrug.

"No, I want a fucking answer. This isn't just a matter of you hiding this from me. You were supposed to trust me, if you ever had a craving, so I could talk you down. This is about respect. For me and especially for Brie."

"I know. I messed up."

"That's not good enough, Mike!" He picks up one of the bottles and throws it at me. It misses and shatters into a hundred shards on the wall. "This isn't about just having one or two drinks. It's about keeping a promise. This means so much more than just drowning out your demons. This is about what our sobriety represents. This is what killed Brie. It's what killed—"

"I know!" I shout back. "I know how bad it is. You think I don't? Especially after you've been here for me, believing in me, every step of the way? You think I didn't want to tell you about this?"

Nate shakes his head, his face dark with fury. "Then why didn't you?"

I try to come up with something, but he is already heading for the door.

"You know what? Fuck this, and fuck you." With that, he storms out of the apartment, slamming the door behind him.

My pulse pounds in my ears. Of everything Chester has done to me, this is by far the worst.

No.

Not Chester.

I did this. Me.

Spontaneous Writing: Session 11

```
Kill Beth
Kill Beth
Kill Beth
Kill Beth
Kill Beth
Kill Beth
Kill Beth
Kill Beth
Kill Beth
Kill Beth
Kill Beth
Kill Beth
Kill Beth
Kill Beth
Kill Beth
Kill Beth
```

CHAPTER 11

I drag myself into the theater, ready to start what will surely be the longest day of tech in my career.

Normally, entering the theater has a bit of magic to it. Up until this point, we have been stuck in a big white box forty feet underground, playing make-believe. But being in the actual space allows the mind to fill in all the gaps which were only dreams before. The set is built, painted, and ready. The props are all laid out. Hundreds of red-velvet seats hum with the spirits of every patron who has ever been here and the thrumming excitement of everyone who will soon watch the culmination of our blood, sweat, and tears.

In this case, literally.

But instead of soaking in the moment and breathing in that familiar and comforting smell of history, I'm scrambling to grab my seat and get moving. Instead of holding the thousand show-related details in my head, I'm repeating the baseline to "Seven Nation Army" over and over with my teeth.

Eden is already in position, and I look around for Nate. He's not here. And he wouldn't answer any of my calls last night or texts this morning. Once again, I was right on the precipice of hope, only to have things come crashing down around me. But this time, I don't have Nate here to put me back together.

Because I have ruined it.

When I spot Bitsie coming down the aisle, I forget all about our pact for public professionalism and squeeze her so tightly I worry she might break.

"Morning, Mike. Are you okay?" she asks. "I heard you upstairs last night while Danny and I were rehearsing. You sounded upset."

"Nate and I had a fight. I'm okay." I try to focus on the one good thing I have now. "You ready for a fun day of standing around under a hot light?"

She gives me a playfully mocking snicker. "Of course! Who doesn't love to soak in the spotlight?"

The day drags, as I expected.

Tech rehearsals aren't even really rehearsals, at least for the actors. It is a long, boring process for them while the crew learns the play, plots out the lighting and sound cues, and practices scene changes. Luckily, our show doesn't have a whole heck of a lot of technical work to do.

We have four sets. First is the doctor's office from the opening scene, which is a sparse layout with just a few cabinets, a prop doctor's chair, and a mirror, where the Wife learns of her miscarriage. Next is the living room of the couple's city home, where the majority of the first act takes place. We have two scenes with Husband at his office, where he cheats on his Wife with The Boss. This set is just a reconfiguration of the doctor's office. Then finally, we have the rural home, which is the only set for Act 2. There are only a few cosmetic changes to that set to make it appear damaged after the storm. This sets up the final scene, in which the couple ponders if the house, as a metaphor for their marriage, can be fixed.

We manage to get it done in one grueling day, but it takes nearly fourteen hours. While there's not much for the actors to do other than hit their marks, there is also a lot of downtime for me to stew in a mire of worry and doubt. I try to occupy myself in the dead moments by studying my lines in the script. After my blowout last night with Nate, I never managed to get around to rehearsing.

By the time the workday ends, everyone is wiped. Bitsie asks if I want to join her and Danny for another run-through tonight, but I am so exhausted from not sleeping yesterday and so ashamed of myself that I turn her down.

It seems even Chester is feeling satisfied. When I get back to my apartment, there is no trace of him. I continue to work on my lines and eat a leftover sandwich for dinner.

Thursday morning comes, our final full day of dress rehearsals. Still no word from Nate.

The crew has to re-do a few transitions. The storm scene is a bit messy due to the quick background change, along with the technical aspects of lightning and thunder. However, much like the sun which shines at the end of the play, we make it through alive.

The only thing really dragging the show down at this point is my performance. My character is only in four scenes, but every time I move from my director's seat next to Eden down to the wings off-stage, I get a sudden urge to pee, and all my lines vanish from my head. I have a hard time sticking to my lighting cues while also spitting out my lines. Never mind putting any actual emotion into it. I'm struggling enough just fumbling my way through the show.

At the end of the day, I feel like a fraud telling everyone they did a great job. Their eyes are filled with concern, not for themselves, not for the lack of appropriate rehearsal time, but for me. Whatever respect they had left has evaporated after watching my horribly crude attempt at acting.

Maybe worst of all is Bitsie. Instead of disappointment, I see pity. It's almost too much for me to take.

When we all break for the day, she offers to have me over to her place for once, to cook me a homemade dinner and coach me through the show ahead of tomorrow's premiere. Despite my exhaustion, I need to take her up on it. We are one night away from opening, and there is no way I can step on stage looking anything like how I did today.

"Forgive the mess. I'm barely ever here," Bitsie says when we walk into her apartment just a few blocks from the theater.

I don't know what I imagined Bitsie's apartment to look like, but it isn't this. I am aware my OCD forces me to live with a certain level of order, but her apartment is a cluttered mess of scripts and books piled up past my head. Half-finished craft projects take up almost every surface, from beaded jewelry to unfinished knitted garments. But while the place may not be tidy, at least I can say it's clean.

There *is* a difference.

An untidy home means unorganized, potentially with some hoarding or careless placement of personal items. An unclean home has old plates of moldy food and cups of curdled milk left around. It has sticky surfaces and a sink whose bottom you can't even find under stacks of dirty dishes. An unclean house has gunk under the toilet seat and a smell that warns of mold and germs.

I can live with an untidy space, even if I do have to fight back a compulsion to organize her scripts and books by size and shape. And I am aware—and have been reminded many times—that my level of tidiness is the exception, not the norm. Long ago, I learned to withhold judgement of other people's homes based on these factors, just as long as they are merely untidy and not unclean.

There is one thing, though, which does strike me as odd. During the short duration of our tour, I don't see a single photograph on the walls. Not with friends, not with family. It makes me realize how little I actually know her. I try to find a way to bring it up without sounding nosey.

"Do you have any family that's coming to see the show?" I ask.

"No," she says, and for a moment, I think she is going to leave it at that. "I was what you might have called a latchkey kid. My mom wasn't in the picture, and my dad worked nights and weekends, which was honestly probably for the best. We never got along."

I want to push further, to ask if he is still alive, but decide to move on. "What about friends? Any ex-boyfriends I need to pretend to be macho in front of?"

She laughs. "You don't have to worry about that. I haven't traditionally been a long-term relationship type of person. And the guys I have dated aren't exactly the tough-guy type." Bitsie gulps, catching herself in what might seem like an overshare, and she doubles back on her words. "Not to say I'm not open to something serious. I just haven't found the right guy yet. Or...who knows?" Her mouth curls up in a smile which accentuates her little round cheeks—the same one that attracted me to her in the first place.

"What about friends?"

She gives me a half shrug. "Most of my friends come and go with each show, and the few folk who live here are also actors, off performing somewhere else. You'll probably meet them at some point during the run, but right now, pretty much everyone I know is out of town. And before you ask, no, I don't have any siblings. I had to learn how to keep myself entertained as a kid. Hours performing stuffed-animal theater in front of a mirror is probably what led me to where I am today."

She walks over to the kitchen, opens the fridge, and pulls out a bottle of wine. Shame sparks through me like a firecracker, and I put up a hand before she can open it.

"I should hold off, at least until the show. I need to stay sharp if I'm going to get this right. As I'm sure you could tell today, I need a lot of work."

In a second, Bitsie has crossed the room and caresses her soft hand against my cheek. "You've got so much to worry about already. Cut yourself some slack. We'll get you there. Trust me."

"I do."

She leans up onto her toes and kisses me slowly and passionately on the lips. It helps ease the tension while I melt into her. But just as soon as I feel myself pulling close, she disengages.

"First, we need to eat. Can't rehearse on an empty stomach. That's rule number one." Bitsie opens the fridge, relieving me of any compulsion to check it myself. She grabs a chicken breast, then pulls a butcher knife from a block on her counter.

When she holds the blade up, lightning flashes in my head and takes me somewhere else. Only this time, instead of having a vision of me killing her, I am instead watching her brandishing the blade in Greenwood Terrace. Her face appears the same but smaller. *Everything* about her is tiny. She is smiling while she takes the knife and drives it into a young boy who must be Caleb.

The little girl then turns to me and licks the blade. Blood runs from her mouth when she asks me, "You like curry?"

I flash back to the present. My pulse quickens. This isn't real. Just another one of Chester's tricks.

"Did I lose you there?" she asks.

"Sorry," I say. "Yeah, just tired. Curry sounds great."

She starts chopping the chicken into bite-sized pieces, and I take another look around her place, announcing that I am going to snoop through her knickknacks. The one spot in her home in which there isn't any clutter is a tiny nook where she keeps a laptop.

Actually, there are *two* laptops.

One is an Acer, while the other is a MacBook propped up against the wall. It has a sticker on it which reads *Murder Mansion*. Each word of the sticker is stacked on top of each other. The font is like a campy '80s movie, and the pair of M's form a gothic-looking spire that ends in a pointed red conical roof.

"What's *Murder Mansion*?" I ask.

Some vague memory of having heard those words ignites. Perhaps I saw that logo before.

"Oh," Bitsie says, suddenly serious. "I have to admit something to you. I am a fan of cheesy horror movies."

Her deadpan delivery earns a genuine guffaw from me, and I fidget around her place a bit more while we chat and she makes dinner.

The curry is delicious. I'm no chef, and this is the first homemade meal I've had in as long as I can remember. Despite my nerves for tomorrow's show, I even venture back to the kitchen to grab a second helping. It's so damned good. While I am at it, I can't help but gently slide my thumb against each of her burners to make sure they are all off.

With our bellies full, we finally move on to rehearsing my parts for the show.

The doctor role I'm able to nail with relative ease. He is meant to be mostly clinical in his delivery anyway, so it doesn't matter that I'm a little stiff. The neighbor, as well, isn't so much a problem. He only pops in a couple of times to welcome the couple to country life and establish a juxtaposition to what they experienced back in the city. Again, it's all right for me to not be terribly good there. He has very little impact on the show.

What gives me trouble are the scenes with Wife's Brother. He is her rock when she learns of her Husband's betrayal, and he is the only one there for her when they uproot their life and she feels like an island due to Husband's growing emotional distance. Not only is it hard for me to get my voice to find the right pacing and tone of the conversation, I can't even keep the lines straight.

"You always know you can come back home, day or night," I say for the fortieth time.

Anyone else's patience would be running on empty by now, but Bitsie just laughs and shakes her head. "I don't know why this one gets you every time. It's 'If you ever want to come back home, you know I'll be there for you, day or night.'"

"Honestly, after doing this, I have a new respect for you managing to learn this all so damn fast."

"You know, if you want to just change it, nobody's going to stop you. I mean, you wrote the damn thing, after all."

I jerk my head back in response to this. it's the second time she has now said this. "I didn't write *Wherever You Go*. Nate did."

She shakes her head, still smiling. "That's not what the script says." She closes her book and shows me the first page. It reads: "Wherever You Go, by Mike O'Brien."

"How bizarre," I note. A tickle of anxiety causes me to huff out a half-chuckle. "Who the heck changed the wording on your version?"

"Speaking of, when am I going to get to meet this mysterious Nate you talk about so much?"

I don't know how to respond to this. Clearly, my face is contorting into something strange. The smile on her face drops to something resembling confusion and concern.

"What? You're kidding, right?" I ask.

Her face is dead serious, and she shakes her head. "Why would I be kidding? Am I missing something?"

"Yeah..." My voice comes out surprisingly hostile. "He's been at almost every rehearsal, sitting right next to me. Tall guy, black hair, with a pointed beard?"

She shakes her head again, a complete lack of recognition in her eyes. "Mike, I have no idea who you're talking about."

For a second, it's like the world flips upside-down. I reach a jittery hand into my pocket, ready to pull out my phone and show her a picture of the Nate and me standing outside the theater ahead of our first day of rehearsal. But when I scroll through, I can't find it.

"No, he's been here the whole time!" I'm shouting now.

Bitsie recoils in fear. She is afraid of me.

Hell, *I* am afraid of me.

I tap his name in my texting app and scroll through our conversation. The air is forced out of my lungs as if I was kicked in the chest. Days, months, of a green wall of my texts scroll ever upward, without a single reply to be found."

"Mike, you're scaring me. What's going on?"

What *is* going on?

Almost in fast-forward, I scan my memories of the past month, of every day I have had with Nate. Not just him, but other odd moments leap out at me. Chester telling me it's not over after I gloated to him that I had confided in Bitsie about Brie. Me telling the story of her death and stopping before I told Bitsie about the aftermath.

My legs shake, and I fall to her couch. My brain feels like a record player with a scratch. Every time I come back to that memory, the needle hits a damaged mark, and I fast-forward.

"I...Oh god."

"What is it?" she asks, starting to step toward me, then thinking better of it and keeping her distance.

"Nate...I remember. After Brie's death. Nate and I, we made a pact that we would stop all the drugs, the drinking, cold turkey. Never again. But then, two days later, I got a call. He was drunk, begging me for help. I wanted to go to him, to be there, but the pain of it all...the guilt. It was too much. I freaked out, got in my car, and left. I abandoned him, drove to California. He called me again just past three in the morning. I was already halfway down the grapevine by then. I wanted to pick up, but...

"I learned the next day he'd committed suicide. Drank himself into a stupor, then lied down in bed and somehow managed to slit his own throat."

My stomach lurches. The world spins. He died the same way as Chester's wife and Alex.

"I have to go."

"Mike, wait!" Bitsie calls, but I throw myself to my feet and out her front door.

I hurry down her stairs, not even counting the steps. Acid roils, and I throw up two plates' worth of curry on the sidewalk.

My whole body is shaking like a leaf while I hurry back to my apartment.

"Why didn't you pick up?" Nate's voice echoes nearby. "I needed you. I *trusted* you. You made a promise."

I glance down an alley and see him standing there, not as the forty-year-old I've been talking to these past weeks, but as the twenty-five-year-old kid who desperately needed help after I killed his sister. Who I failed.

How long have I been suppressing this? Have I been hallucinating him this whole time? Or is he another ghost tethered to this place and haunting me until I confront my demons?

"I'm sorry, Nate. I'm so, so sorry," I plead, running my forearm against the tears and snot pouring down my face. "How could I have forgotten?"

"You needed me. I didn't want to let you down. I saw the path you were headed on and didn't want you to end up like me."

"What are you?" I beg when he reappears right in front of me. "Are you in my head? Are you a ghost? Tell me!"

"Doesn't matter," he says. "As long as I got you here. And you were doing so well, even dealing with Chester..."

"Chester!" Holy hell. My mind races back to the morning in the café, when Nate told me the story of Chester. He confirmed all my beliefs that Chester was a ghost. Made me feel sane when I thought I was losing my mind. "Is Chester real?"

Nate shrugs. "I don't know. Is he?"

I pull out my phone and call Eden.

"What is it, Mike?" she asks.

"Chester Mays. I asked you the other day if you knew the story of Chester Mays."

"Yeah, he was an amazing director. Everyone knows about him."

"Was he murdered?"

A pause. "What?" she asks.

"What happened to him? To Chester Mays? Was he murdered here in Seattle?"

"I don't know. It was before my time. There are rumors, but I don't know any specifics. What's going on?"

I hang up the phone, and it immediately buzzes. Eden is calling me back, but I ignore it and round the corner to Greenwood Terrace. At the top of the stairs, I pound on Chester's door, peer through his window.

Nothing.

I go to my apartment and pull the door shut.

"Chester, are you here?" I ask. "Chester, come out, you son of bitch!"

I sit down at my desk, pull my computer from my shoulder bag, and open it up to my spontaneous writing doc.

Spontaneous Writing: Session 12

Chester where are you?
Chester, talk to me
Carrots and Brie
Carrots and Brie
Chester, fucking talk to me!
Chester, I need you to tell me the
Mikey boy, welcome back. I was wondering when you'd finally listen.
You want answers? I need you to do something for me first.
And no, I'm not going to ask you to Kill Beth.
I have a new task for you.
Look up Murder Mansion, then you'll understand.

CHAPTER 12

I wake up, sitting in front of my laptop. The clock reads 3:14 a.m. The words are there on the screen. What else am I to do but follow Chester's command?

I open Google and type in the words "Murder Mansion."

What pops up is a movie from 2014 based on a true story of a serial killer named Arthur Wilson. My heart nearly stops when I discover two things in quick succession.

The first is that the movie starred Landon Keating, the brother of our former lead actor, Alex Keating. The second is the picture of Landon in the poster. He's wearing glasses and a brown checkered coat. It's not quite the same as Chester, but similar enough that, at first glance, I nearly have a heart attack. I think back to the picture of Chester in the rehearsal hall and the ghost story I am not certain I remember hearing all those years ago. Could I really have made all this up?

No, of course not. The details Chester knew...He has been right about so many things. There is no way I invented him. Nate might be in my head, but Chester is real.

And then it hits me. The connection.

I fly out the door and nearly trip heading down the stairs. A spark flashes through my head. More lost time. The next thing I know, I'm back inside Bitsie's apartment. She stands across from me, her beautiful blue eyes huge and glassy in terror.

"I said, what are you doing here?" she asks, as if we are already mid-conversation.

I shake my head and try to get my bearings. There is something in my hand.

The laptop with the *Murder Mansion* sticker.

"Where did you get this?" I ask.

"It's just an old—"

"Don't lie to me!" I demand. "Did you steal this from Alex Keating? Did *you* kill him?"

Her mouth opens and closes several times. It takes her what feels like a minute before she responds.

"No, it's just my old computer. You can open it if you want. You'll see it's full of my stuff."

I don't know how I know, but I can tell she's lying.

"I don't believe you, Beth."

Her cheeks flush bright red. She looks at me as if I just slapped her in the face.

"What did you call me?"

"Why? What does it mean to you if I call you Beth?"

Beth shakes her head and stumbles a few steps backward toward her bedroom. "Nobody's called me that since I was a child. Not since I—"

"Since you killed Chester Mays?"

She hiccups out a tear. Her frail body trembles. "I've never killed anyone. That's insane."

"Then why did you change your name to Bitsie? Why not Beth?"

"I told you, I had a bad relationship with my father. He used to call me Beth. I emancipated myself at sixteen, and I've gone by Bitsie ever since."

"Did you ever spend any time at Greenwood Terrace as a kid?"

"I mean, yeah, a little. I told you I was on my own a lot. Sometimes, people came through and they had kids. Maybe that's what got me interested in theater in the first place."

"That's not what you said before!" I shout. "You said it was from playing with stuffed animals in front of your mirror!"

Tears stream down her face. "I don't know what you want me to say."

All the pieces finally fall into place. Chester has been right all along. Alex's missing laptop, now found...Beth admitting she went to the apartments as a kid...She even knows Steve, the vagrant. I imagine it didn't take her much convincing to get him to break into Alex's apartment and kill him. Beth already confided he saved her once, and he told me he would kill for me over something as simple as clearing up what seemed, at the time, like a minor misunderstanding.

I am *not* crazy. Chester had me writing her name long before I met her. Warned me of her before I could have possibly learned about any of this. There are just too many coincidences. Too much advanced knowledge I couldn't have had without outside intervention.

I reach into my pocket, feel something encrusted in dirt, and pull it out. It's a knife with dirt packed into silver etchings and a faded picture of an eagle holding an American flag in its beak. Steve's knife. I don't know how I got it. It wasn't in my pocket when I left my apartment.

At least, I don't think it was.

I flick the blade out. It's already coated in dried blood.

"Where did this come from?" I ask her. "Was this in your apartment?"

"Mike, please," she begs.

I take a step toward Beth, but within the blink of an eye, Nate appears next to her.

"Come on, man. Don't do this."

Something in my head short-circuits, and a tremble works its way through every muscle of my body.

"What the fuck are you doing here, Nate?"

"What's going on?" Beth glances in the direction of the figure she clearly can't see.

"Just put the knife down, Mike. Come on. I'm here for you."

"Here for me?" Confusion swirls while I think back to our last blowout. "The last thing you did was throw a bottle at me and storm off." Another realization hits me like a truck. "And that whole freakout at seeing Chester…That wasn't real. It was all a show. You two are in it together to fuck with me!"

Nate shakes his head. "It's not like that, man. I was just trying to help you."

"How? You knew I was drinking the whole time! You had to. Why blow up at me like that? I've been feeling like shit for days!"

Nate mocks me with a face of concern. "You think you would have stopped if I just casually told you I knew you were drinking? It's not like I planned anything. I didn't know Chester was coming. When I saw the bottles, it just came up as the perfect opportunity to, I don't know, get you back on the right path."

I am trying to process his words, but Beth keeps crying and pleading over him, and it is making my head spin.

"I was going to come back." Nate says. "You were doing so well. I just want to see you get better. You gotta believe me. I've always been on your side."

"On my side? You're dead!" I shout back. Hot streaks of tears slice down my cheeks. "I don't *want* you on my side. I don't *want* to see Chester haunting me in the middle of the night. I didn't *want* to come back here in the first place. I just wanted to be left alone!"

Spit flies from my mouth while I bark through gritted teeth. It will do no good, but I lunge toward Nate, swiping the knife at him. It passes through empty air.

From my periphery comes swift movement.

Beth darts across the room, and I spin around. She pulls a kitchen knife from her block. Her breath is heaving, and her quivering arm holds out the blade, protecting her tiny frame.

"Please! Don't do this. You're really scaring me." She hiccups through a river of tears.

Cigarette smoke wafts through the air. Her knife drips with blood, and her apartment has transformed. We're back in Greenwood Terrace. Beth stands between the bodies of Chester and his son, with a woman lying dead on a bed behind her.

I try to blink away the vision, but another searing bolt hits my brain like lightning.

The next thing I know, I'm lying in her bed. My phone is buzzing.

"Hello?"

"Where the hell are you, Mike?" Eden screams into the receiver. "We've been calling you and Bitsie all day! It's nearly thirty minutes to curtain, and you're not here!"

I check the time on my phone. She's right. Nearly a whole day has passed in a flash.

Next to me is the body.

Her dark hair is matted over her porcelain skin. Her once bright blue eyes have lost their light and stare up at the ceiling in a pale gray. Those cheeks which plumped up in such a cute way every time she smiled are thin and slack. Her mouth hangs open, just like the deep gash traced across her throat.

I am naked, except for my underwear. We are both covered in blood. It's cold, sticky, mostly dry.

In this moment, I realize there is no coming back from what I have done. The jig is up, so to speak. I can't run this time, like I did to Nate, and I have no other option but to face what has happened head-on.

"I'm so sorry," I say into the phone. "I'll be right over."

I shower Beth's blood off me. Even after covering myself in shampoo and soap multiple times, traces of red still swirl down the drain. When I am done, I find my clothes scattered around the floor and get dressed. I search through her closet for a trench coat to cover the bloodstains on my shirt.

I stare at the body on the bed. It appears just like Chester's wife, just how I imagine Nate looked when he took his own life. It feels as though the whole building is crumbling around me. There are no more scapegoats, no one else to blame. *I* did this. Bitsie is dead because of me. Because she trusted me.

I have failed not just her, but everyone. So many people on so many levels. As the director, it was my job to keep everyone safe. To be the one figure they believed in. Instead, I held Brie's hand and dragged her toward her death. I abandoned Nate when he needed me most. Stood by and watched Cassandra get mutilated. I still don't even know if I killed Alex. And now, Bitsie.

I have also effectively killed the show. All the other people who relied on me, respected me...I have let everyone down. This, I tell myself, this is what happens when I get close to the cast. When I climb down from my tower of isolation and try to pretend like I am a human being. People die, and it's my fault.

On a table in front of me sits the MacBook Bitsie swore was hers. I approach it with caution, as if it were on fire, and open it up. A prompt for a password appears, and behind it is a picture of Bitsie standing on a stage with a group of people who I assume are old castmates. She wasn't lying. This is her laptop, not Alex Keatings's.

It doesn't matter if he was a ghost or a hallucination. Nate was wrong about me. There is no redemption, no path to live a normal life from here. All that is left for me is to do the responsible thing, the only thing left that matters.

I hurry to The Burgess.

"Where the hell have you been?" Eden asks when I push my way toward my dressing room.

"I'm so sorry, for everything I've put you through. I promise, I'm going to make it right as best I can. I need to get on stage. You'll understand soon."

"This isn't okay, Mike. After this, we're having a serious talk with Rebecca."

I nod. An overwhelming sense of calm washes over me. "Okay."

I enter my changing room. My clothes are wrinkled, and my shirt is covered in blood. I trade it for my costume. Even after the shower, when I stare into the mirror, I can still see traces of crimson on my face.

I grab the stage makeup kit and start using some to cover up the stains. It is my first time applying stage makeup, but I know the basics. If I am going to go out there and address all these people, I might as well do it in the appropriate way. When I am finished, I traverse the small labyrinth backstage, fumble my way through the darkness, and stand behind the curtain.

Inside the theater is the constant din of chatter from the audience. By the sound of it, we have a packed house, here to watch the culmination of my life's work. A nervous energy permeates the building, making it hum with anticipation.

Next to me is a glowing red cherry of a cigarette. Chester joins me on stage, smiling.

"I told you this wasn't over."

Before I can respond, Eden's voice echoes throughout the theater, informing patrons to turn off their cellphones and refrain from any flash photography during the show. She then welcomes everyone to The Burgess's production of *Wherever You Are*.

An ominous musical sting leads into the opening scene. The curtain rises. Chester's form is swallowed by the climbing light until all that is left is a vague odor of smoke.

I nearly jump when, behind me, Danny starts the play off with his first line.

"This is taking forever," he says.

"Would you relax? Stressing more isn't going to help the doctor come in any sooner," Wife responds, hopping up from the doctor's table and walking over to the mirror.

"How's your stomach? Are you feeling any better?" His delivery is strange, and it is only when Wife gazes into the mirror that I realize why.

My reflection is nothing like how I saw myself in the dressing room. My face looks like a kid went nuts on a doll with face paint. My lipstick is crudely carved across not just my lips, but smeared all the way up my cheeks, making me resemble the Joker. My eyes are buried in black which streaks into my crow's feet. I have so much foundation on I look like a ghost.

Not a real ghost because I know they look just like people. More like the kind from a movie.

In order to work my way into Bitsie's costume, I've had to tear it apart on nearly every seam. The neck forms a deep V down my chest, the shoulders are in tatters, and one arm is missing completely. My wig is askew. Dark shoulder-length hair sits lopsided on my head.

I turn to the audience. "Stop worrying, already. I'm sure I'm fine."

But it's *not* fine. Nothing will ever be fine again. Even with Bitsie gone, I somehow believed I could still salvage the evening. But the show cannot go on. Not this time.

I know what I have to do now.

In my hand is the dirty switchblade covered in the crusted blood of two people. I raise it to my throat, and the lights cut out.

About the Author

Jon Cohn is a horror novelist and professional board game designer. His works include 2024 Indie Book Brawl Quarter-Finalist *Slashtag*, and the much less popular, but award winning novel *The Island Mother*. He gets his best ideas from a tarot reader who lives in Hawaii.

As a designer, Jon is very excited to finally be able to merge horror books and games together by bringing *Ghostland* to life as a board game, coming to Kickstarter. He's also designed games like *Thanksgiving*, co-designed with Eli Roth, *Basket Case*, and *Taboo Horror*.

Order autographed books, and get updates for new games and upcoming novels at www.joncohnauthor.com. Sign up for the newsletter for free short stories and games, and follow at @joncohnauthor on Facebook, Instagram and TikTok .

Jon lives in San Diego with his supernaturally patient wife Delaney, and their adorable dog, Miss Cordelia Chase.

www.ingramcontent.com/pod-product-compliance
Lightning Source LLC
Chambersburg PA
CBHW060417310726
48976CB00003B/1092